Cold Blooded

Cold Blooded

Roy Glenn

www.urbanbooks.net

Urban Books, LLC
300 Farmingdale Road, N.Y.-Route 109
Farmingdale, NY 11735

ISBN 13: 978-1-64556-397-6
ISBN 10: 1-64556-397-9

First Trade Paperback Printing January 2023
Printed in the United States of America

10 9 8 7 6 5 4 3 2 1

*This is a work of fiction. Any references or similarities
to actual events, real people, living or dead, or to real
locales are intended to give the novel a sense of reality.
Any similarity in other names, characters, places, and
incidents is entirely coincidental.*

Distributed by Kensington Publishing Corp.
Submit Orders to:
Customer Service
400 Hahn Road
Westminster, MD 21157-4627
Phone: 1-800-733-3000
Fax: 1-800-659-2436

Cold Blooded

by

Roy Glenn

Chapter One

The Playhouse was a nightclub and gambling house run by Barbara Ray. But it wasn't always the Playhouse. Before Barbara took over, the name of the spot was Sweet Nectar. The Nectar, as many had called it over the years, was located in her father's old neighborhood. Like the Nectar, the neighborhood was changing, meaning a new drug gang had forced their way in. Now those corners belonged to them.

The gang called themselves the G40s. They were expanding, and not just drug territory. The G40s were moving into extortion and protection rackets. It was the same old game that had been run for years—local merchants paid the gang to leave them alone so they could operate their business without disturbance from the gang. What bigger prize was there than the Nectar? It was a neighborhood institution. And now that it was called the Playhouse, it was one that Rawdawg, the leader of the G40s, had to have. Especially after he'd heard from so many people how fine the woman who ran the Playhouse was.

It started out as simple vandalism. The neon Playhouse sign in front of the building and a few windows were broken, and some customers got harassed outside. There was some shooting a couple of nights later when two of the G40s, who had come there that night to shake them down for protection money, tried to get into the Playhouse and were refused entry. A sit-down request was made by the G40s to settle the matter but was ignored. As a result, the vandalism intensified, and minor skirmishes outside the club continued. Although they were an annoyance, their activities hadn't risen to a level where anybody felt that it needed to be brought to Barbara's attention. That happened when three G40s caught the head server, Ishawna Patrick, coming out of the club one morning after the Playhouse closed. They kidnapped her and held her at gunpoint in one of their apartments. She was released unharmed a few hours later. The purpose of the kidnapping was to deliver a message.

A sit-down was promptly arranged for the following evening.

As head of security at the Playhouse, Axe Bryson arranged for Barbara to meet unarmed with Rawdawg. Each would be permitted to have three of their people with them. At seven o'clock, Rawdawg and his men arrived at the Playhouse for their long-awaited sit-down with Barbara. To them, the sit-down meant that Barbara had capitulated, and they were there to arrogantly dictate terms. They were met at the door by Garrett, one of Barbara's personal bodyguards. He searched each man before he allowed them to enter the Playhouse. When they stepped inside, Axe was waiting for them.

"Right this way," Axe said, waving them over to the table where the sit-down was to take place.

He was standing next to Barbara's personal bodyguard, Tahanee Stevens. When Barbara was kidnapped during Rona King's proxy war with The Family, it was Tahanee who saved her.

"Damn," Rawdawg said, looking at Tahanee. "Look at you." He took a few steps toward the table. "I heard a sexy-ass bitch ran this place."

"You need to shut the fuck up and sit your bitch ass down," Tahanee said.

"What your bitch ass gonna do if I don't?"

"She's not going to do anything."

All eyes turned to see Barbara, standing with her fists balled against her hips. "She doesn't run this place. I do."

Barbara walked toward the table wearing a black David Koma one-shoulder minidress with crystal-embellished tank straps that hugged her curves like a second skin.

"Shit, your muthafuckin' ass even finer than that bitch there." Rawdawg stepped up to the table and put his hands on the chair. "Shit, goddamn, you got the whole muthafuckin' show working for you, sexy. All of them hips and thighs and shit. Turn around, sexy, and let me see you bounce that ass for a nigga."

Barbara ignored his vulgar request and kept walking. *As if I were actually gonna do that shit.* When she got to the table, Axe pulled out her chair, and in the most ladylike manner she could muster, Barbara sat down at the table.

"Not gonna show me that phat ass, huh?" He chuckled and sat down. "That's all right, sexy. Bouncing them pretty-ass titties for a nigga when you sat down was good enough." He licked his lips. "Yeah, sexy, me and you gonna get along real good."

Barbara shook her head in disgust. "Is that all you came here to say?"

Rawdawg leaned forward quickly.

Barbara didn't flinch.

"No, sexy." Rawdawg leaned back slowly. "I came to tell your sexy muthafuckin' ass that you're gonna pay me two grand a week, cash money. We not gonna have no more problems at the door with my niggas getting in. Ain't no more age limit for them. And your sexy muthafuckin' ass gonna put that money in my muthafuckin' hand personally," he said, pointing to the palm of his hand. He sat back. "You do that, like a good little bitch, and I might even let you have some of this dick," he said, reaching under the table to grab it. "And I know your sexy mutha-fuckin' ass gonna love it."

Once again, Barbara shook her head in disgust. "Are you finished?"

"Yeah, sexy." He smiled and nodded his head. "I think that covers it."

"Good. First off, what you said to me was offensive. It was crude and disgusting. If my father or my brother were here, or my uncle Mike, they would have killed you for disrespecting me."

"I'm scared." Rawdawg looked around and laughed, as did the three men who had come with him.

"Now to the matter of me paying you for protection. Let me make you a counteroffer," Barbara said. Then she folded her hands in front of her.

"What's your offer, sexy?"

"Did you hear me say anything?"

"No."

"Then that must be my offer. Nothing."

Rawdawg looked confused. "Nothing?"

"Nothing. Nada, zilch, zip," Barbara said, leaning slowly forward. "My personal check for zero dollars from the First National Bank of I Ain't Giving You a Muthafuckin' Thing," she said, reaching under the table. She got the Glock 42 from her thigh holster. Barbara stood up and shot Rawdawg twice in the head.

When she did, Tahanee, Garrett, and Axe took out their weapons and killed the three men who'd come with Rawdawg.

"Call Edwina," Barbara said, handing Axe her gun. She went back into her office with Tahanee.

Their bodies were taken to the Parlor for disposal in the crematorium.

Chapter Two

Black was in the basement at Bobby's house with him and Wanda. He asked her to meet them there so they could talk about something important. Without his knowledge, Rain, Jackie, and Carter had participated in the murder of Greg Mac and Drum for Gavin Caldwell. He found out when he returned from vacation, and Angelo told him about the task force having a witness who had identified the killers as Gavin Caldwell and a woman in a blond wig and sunglasses.

"Have you talked to her about it?" Wanda asked.

"Not yet."

"Are you going to?" she asked.

"Or are you gonna put her through one of your damn tests to test her judgment?" Bobby asked.

"You know, Bob, that's not a bad idea," Black said and got up to pour another drink.

"By the way, Mike, I was sorry to hear about Quentin," Wanda said.

"Thanks, Wanda."

Earlier that day, Black and Shy attended the funeral of his friend Quentin Hunter. He had been shot to death in the home of his friend and business associate, Daniel Beason, who, despite claiming to be innocent of the murder, fled the scene before the police arrived.

"Have the police found Beason yet?" she asked.

Black sat down. "No, they haven't, but Ebony doesn't think he did it," he said and looked at Bobby. "I was thinking about, you know, asking a few questions."

"You want some company?" Bobby asked.

Black smiled. "Always."

"Oh, no," Wanda said and sipped her apple martini. "The two of you, back in the streets."

"Don't call it a comeback, Wanda," Bobby said and fist-bumped Black.

Wanda shook her head. "What happened with Beason and Colton anyway?"

"It all started when Elias Colton was murdered." Black chuckled. "Somebody threw him off the balcony of his midtown condo."

"Sounds like something you and Bobby would do," Wanda said and laughed.

"Probably why the cops wanted to talk to you about the murder," Bobby said, and he laughed too.

"No, that wasn't it at all. Detective Mitchell wanted to know if I would be her murder consultant."

"You're kidding."

"No, Wanda, she was dead serious. She said that she needs to understand how a killer thinks." Black paused. "And let's face it—I am qualified."

"Understanding killers would make her a better detective," Wanda said.

"That's what I told her, but I'm guessing that she already knew that and that's why she asked me."

"What did you tell her about Elias Colton's murder?"

"I told her that I thought Albert and Gayle looked good for it, but it was deeper than that."

"Why did you think that it was deeper than that?"

"Because Albert is too big a pussy to even think about killing Elias."

"Not very scientific."

"But it does have the advantage of being true. They eliminated Albert and Gayle as suspects, and it was much deeper than Elias fucking Gayle."

"So what was it about?"

"I don't know for sure, but Quentin said it was about some failed land deal that the three of them were involved in years ago. But I don't think that's what it was about."

"What do you think it is?"

"Quentin mentioned to me once that Beason had asked if he wanted to invest in a new shipping venture with him and Elias and promised that he would be able to more than quadruple his money within a year."

"Something illegal, I'm sure," Wanda said. And she would know. She was the mastermind behind The Family's financial success, or as Nick once called her, Wanda was the mad scientist who made everybody rich.

"Quentin said that when he asked what they would be shipping, Beason said that it's best not to ask." Black paused. "Beason said all Quentin needed to know was that his money was guaranteed."

"So where were you thinking about starting?" Wanda asked.

"Quentin said that he met them at a bar in Queens called Tirana. I think that's as good a place as any to start."

Bobby shook his head. "That is all well and good, but I want to know what you're gonna do about Rain."

"I don't know, Bob. What do you think I should do?"

"I think you should exile her to an island in the Bahamas. You know, the way the two of you did to me," Wanda said, and Bobby pointed at Black. "No, Bobby. Don't point at Mike. You were as much a part of my exile as he was."

"First of all, you were on that island for a reason."

Wanda waved her hand dismissively. "Whatever, Mike."

"No, Wanda!" He pointed in her face. "You made an enemy of the wrong muthafucka. He had already beheaded Richie, and the men he sent almost killed you! There was no way I was going to leave you in some fuckin' hospital and wait for him to send men to finish the job! Like it or not, you were safer on that island. And I am not going to apologize for trying to keep somebody from killing you."

"And I am not asking you to apologize!" Wanda said, rocking her head from side to side with each word. "All I want you to do is acknowledge that at some point it became a punishment that fit your needs."

"What?" an obviously confused Black asked.

"It was working for you to make everybody think that you had killed me!"

"Not that it mattered. It just drove muthafuckas underground," Bobby said.

Wanda held up her hand. "Not the point."

"What's the point?"

"The point is that it was working for you! If it weren't for Shy, I would probably still be down there!"

"Okay, Wanda! Yes, it started out as a way to protect you, and it turned into a punishment that worked out great for us," he said sarcastically and then turned to Bobby. "Driving them underground was what led to you getting shot."

"And to Cynt getting killed," Bobby happily added.

"And all that is on me. I fucked up." Wanda paused and sipped her drink. "But thank you for admitting it was a punishment. Now I am willing to admit that the punishment was justified. It was just too damn long, but it was justified."

Black looked at Wanda. "After all that, after all this time, it was justified? Is that what you're saying to me?"

"Yes, Mike, it was justified. I just needed you to admit it was a punishment."

"You know, this is all well and good." Bobby shook his head. "I'm glad you admitted you kicked her ass, and I'm glad you admitted that you needed your ass kicked." He got up and walked to the bar. "But I want to know what you're gonna do about Rain."

"You already got my vote," Wanda said, and then she got up to refresh her drink. "Caribbean exile."

Bobby poured both himself and Wanda drinks, and he sat down.

"I'll talk to her. I'll decide what to do about it then." Black smiled. "Unless you wanna call it a comeback and take the reins."

"Fuck no. I don't want her job."

Wanda sat down smiling because, after all she had just said about Caribbean exile, she was about to throw some shit into the conversation. "What did you do to Bobby when he did the same thing with Leon and actually did involve us in a drug war?"

Black looked at Wanda. "I didn't do anything."

"No, you didn't. You just told him that you wouldn't have backed Leon and you went to war with Rico."

"I thought you voted for Caribbean exile," Bobby said.

"I did, but the punishment doesn't fit the crime. Even though she backed Gavin's play, Rain avoided getting us in the middle of his war with Kojo, and she kept us off the task force's radar."

"I agree, but there is still something that she has to answer to me for," Black said.

"What's that?" Bobby asked.

"She should have told me," Black said and finished his drink.

Chapter Three

"You ready to get outta here?"

"Yeah." Bobby shot his drink and stood up. "Where we going?"

"Tirana." Black stood up.

Wanda did too. "Mind if I ride?" she asked.

"Yes!" Bobby said quickly.

"Not at all." Black smiled. "You armed?"

"No," she answered.

Black turned to Bobby. "Give her a gun."

"You sure?"

"About giving her a gun?"

"No, about her coming with us."

"Why don't you want me to come with you two, Bobby?" Wanda asked as Bobby went to get her a gun.

"Because I don't want anything to happen to you," Bobby said, coming back into the room and handing her a Ruger LCP .380. He thought about losing Vickie. "So forgive me for being protective of you."

"I can take care of myself," Wanda said as she followed Black up the stairs. "I think I proved that a long time ago."

"She has, Bob. Wanda's a soldier," Black said and left the house.

"This coming from the guy who used to argue with her during shootouts," Bobby laughed. He closed and locked the door.

Wanda laughed thinking about the pearl-handle .25 she used to carry. "What did I tell you about carrying a gun?" she said, imitating Black's voice.

"I'll be the first one to admit that I was overprotective of you," he said and put his arm around her as they walked. "Especially after Vickie. But like you said, you proved that you could take care of yourself."

"Thank you, Mike," Wanda said as they got to their cars and their bodyguards.

"Mr. Nesmith, how are you, sir?" Black said and shook his hand.

"I'm doing fine, sir," the mountain of a man said.

"Is Ms. West in the city and nobody told me?" he asked because Mr. Nesmith was Jada's personal bodyguard and driver.

When armed gunmen opened fire on Jada and Carmen Taylor, Mr. Nesmith shielded them with his body in order to protect the ladies as they ran for cover. Although he was wearing a vest that night at Enzo's Palace, Mr. Nesmith still took several shots to his arms, and his neck and head were grazed.

"No, sir, Ms. West is in Nassau. However, when Ms. Moore said that she was coming to New York and she didn't have anyone to drive for her, Ms. West insisted that I accompany Ms. Moore on her trip."

"I see." Black turned to William. "I'm gonna ride with Bobby tonight."

"Yes, sir," William said happily and began thinking about how he was going to spend his night off.

"I'm going to be riding with Mr. Ray as well, Mr. Nesmith."

He shook his head. "Ms. West was quite clear in her instructions that I should drive for you."

"If you like, I could call Ms. West for you," Black offered, and Nesmith smiled.

"That won't be necessary, Mr. Black. I'll tell Ms. West that Ms. Moore was with you, and that will end the conversation." He turned to Wanda and bowed at the waist. "Enjoy your evening, Ms. Moore."

"I will call you in the morning when I'm ready to be picked up," Wanda said to Mr. Nesmith as Bobby pulled up in his car.

"As you wish," Mr. Nesmith said. He got into the car he'd rented, thinking about Ymani and how he was going to spend his night off with her.

Black opened the door for Wanda, and then he got into the back seat. "How long are you gonna be in New York?"

"I don't know, a couple of days maybe."

"You are coming to Venus's baby shower, aren't you?" Bobby asked.

"If not, I'll be back in time for her shower. You know I wouldn't miss that," Wanda said, and then she paused. "I gotta say, I love it down there in Nassau, but I miss New York, and I really miss you two."

"I miss you too, Wanda," Bobby said.

"So do I. More than you know," Black concurred.

"That's why I wanted to ride with you two tonight. Most times when I'm in the city, either I'm busy or you two are busy."

"You are always welcome to ride." Black laughed. "You're the third man."

"What?" Wanda questioned.

"You remember the day we were going to rob three-quarters of a million dollars in uncut diamonds that diamond wholesaler had chained to his wrist?"

"And Wanda showed up that morning," Bobby said and laughed. "I remember."

"Dressed in black, talking about we needed another man on the job," Black said, and Wanda laughed because she remembered that day too. "That was the day you showed me that you could take care of yourself," he said, remembering the day that he stepped out into the street, raised the grenade launcher, and fired at the limousine that the diamond wholesaler was in. When the limo swerved at the last second, the grenade hit another car, and it burst into flames. Then Black watched Wanda come roaring through the flames and stay right on their tail. As Wanda closed the distance, Bobby kept firing out the window at the limo. Black pulled up alongside them and began firing out his window until his gun was empty. Then he stepped on the gas and rammed the limo from the back. The limo swerved but recovered quickly and kept going. Wanda pulled up alongside the limo and rammed it while Black rammed it again from the back. When Wanda hit the limo again, it fishtailed and crashed into the cars parked along the street. When the driver opened his door, Bobby shot him. Black brought his car to a screeching halt. He shot one of the bodyguards, and Bobby shot the other. Wanda got out with the bolt cutters to cut the chain.

"Seriously, Wanda, what did you do with your share of the money?" Bobby asked as he did that night when they went to Sherman's house to get paid.

"I really did invest it." Wanda looked back at Black. "How exactly did I prove that I could take care of myself that day?"

"I'd like to hear this too," Bobby said.

"Because anybody can get off a few shots in a firefight. They might even hit something, but that day you showed me that you could handle yourself under pressure." Black laughed. "The plan had gone to shit."

"Damn sure did," Bobby laughed.

"I remember saying to myself, 'Why can't shit ever go the way we plan it?'"

"By not planning the job at the last minute," Wanda laughed.

"It was your plan, Wanda," Bobby said.

"No, it wasn't. My plan was done when your girl got mad because I was with you."

"She's right, Bob, but that proves my point. Whatever plan there was, was gone, and she still stepped up and handled herself," Black said as they arrived at Tirana.

"Tirana is a gentlemen's club? Really?" Wanda asked as they walked up to the building.

"I didn't know," Black said and chuckled.

"You still wanna go in?" Bobby asked as Wanda grabbed the handle.

"Let's go," Wanda said and held the door open for them to go inside. "This ain't my first tittie bar." The three stepped inside and looked around.

"'Not a very popular place with the brothers,'" Bobby said, quoting Eddie Murphy in *48 Hrs*.

"No, it's not," Black said. "Let's get a drink."

"No," Wanda said. "You two get a table. I'll go to the bar."

"Why?" Bobby asked.

"Because they'll talk to me before they talk to either of you," she said and walked off.

"She's right," Black said and looked around for a table where he could see the exits and keep his eyes on Wanda at the same time.

As Wanda went to the bar, Black and Bobby found a table and sat down. As they waited for a server, Black listened to the people speaking around him. It took him a while, but he soon recognized the dialect.

"Albanians."

"What?" Bobby said over the music.

Black leaned closer. "These are Albanians."

"Albanians and shipping." Bobby looked around. "Now we know what illegal shit Beason was into."

"And what got Elias killed, fuckin' with these mutha-fuckas. Ain't no telling what they were shipping."

"Drugs, guns, people, take your pick," Bobby said, keeping his eyes on Wanda at the bar. She had ordered a drink, and the bartender had just placed it in front of her when a man came and stood next to her.

"Your money is no good here, pretty lady," the man said in a distinct Tosk dialect spoken by southern Albanian groups.

"That's all right. I can pay for my own drink, thank you," Wanda said but made no move to do so.

"No, pretty lady, I must insist," he said and dropped a twenty on the bar, which the bartender quickly snatched and moved on. "Now we are friends."

"Look, it's not like that. I just came here looking for a friend I'm supposed to be meeting here."

He tapped his chest. "I am here all the time. I know everybody. What is friend's name?"

"Daniel Beason. Do you know him?"

"I told you, I know everybody, but I am afraid that this man you are looking for, this Daniel Beason, has stood you up this evening. Although I cannot imagine why anyone would miss a chance to be with you, pretty lady."

"Are you sure he's not here?"

"When Daniel Beason is here, Lendina is here. Lendina is not here. Daniel Beason is not here."

Wanda smiled because she had gotten what she wanted, and now it was time to go. She looked at Black and Bobby and nodded.

"Come on, let's go rescue Wanda," Black said and stood up.

He and Bobby walked through the crowd to the bar. When they got to the bar, Bobby stood next to Wanda, and Black stood behind the man she was talking to.

"What's up?" Bobby asked, looking at the man.

"This guy said that Beason isn't here," Wanda said to Bobby, pointing over her shoulder at the man.

"Then we should go," Black said from behind the man, and it startled him.

"Thanks for the drink," Wanda said and followed Black and Bobby away from the bar and out of the club.

"What'd you get?" Black asked as they walked away from Tirana Gentlemen's Club.

"He said that when Beason comes there, he always meets with somebody named Lendina. I don't know if that's a first name, last name, or what, but these are Albanians, Mike," Wanda said as they walked. "Shipping and more than quadrupling his money, we're talking human trafficking."

"We've got company," Bobby said when he noticed that four men had come out of the club and were following them.

"Hey, *njeri i zi*," one said. "Hey, black man."

"Ready?" Black asked, reaching for his gun.

"Give me a second," Wanda said taking the .380 from her clutch. "Got it," she said, and all three turned around with their guns raised.

The men stopped and raised their hands.

"No trouble, no trouble," one said, and he stepped to the front. His name was Lulc Vata. He owned Tirana and was the Kryetar of the Troka Clan.

"What do you want?" Black asked. "Give Wanda your gun and go get the car, Bobby," he said softly. He handed Wanda the gun and rushed off.

"You are looking for Daniel Beason. I am looking for Daniel Beason," he said, lowering his hands slightly.

"When I see him, I'll tell him that you're looking for him," Black said.

"Thank you, but I am interested to hear why you are looking for him."

"Fuck do you care?" Black asked as Bobby pulled up in the car and got out. Wanda handed him back his gun and got in.

"I have business with him."

Now that Wanda was in the car, Black started for it. "Like I said, I'll let him know when I see him."

"I have a feeling that you and I will see each other again."

"And I'll be waiting for you," Black said and got in the car.

Chapter Four

It had been a long couple of days for Carter Garrison. Since Rain told him that she was pregnant and that he was the father, nothing had gone his way. At this point, she was barely speaking to him, and he had no idea where she was. He had been to J.R.'s, and to both her house and her safe house, and Rain was nowhere to be found. And now she wasn't even taking his calls.

"It's about business," Carter said aloud as the call went to voicemail.

Black had tasked Jackie with finding out everything about Kojo and his operation. Kordell Jones aka Kojo met Johnny Boy in the yard while he was serving a fifteen-year sentence for murder and Johnny Boy was serving time for a parole violation. Kojo was telling his fellow inmates why he was in there. Johnny Boy, who was sitting on the benches nearby with some other Italians, heard what he said and told Kojo that he was in there because he was stupid. Everybody laughed, except Kojo of course. He had walked over to where Johnny Boy was sitting. Everything got quiet as all braced for a confrontation.

"Teach me not to be stupid ever again."

Once again, everybody but Kojo laughed, but this time Johnny Boy wasn't laughing either. Instead, he had said, "I like you, kid."

The laughter continued, and Kojo walked away with his head in his hand, but the next day on the yard,

Johnny Boy came and sat down next to him and told him why he was stupid. After that, Kojo became Johnny Boy's student. Within a week, he had a lawyer working on his appeal and got his conviction overturned on a technicality.

After serving only four months of a fifteen-year sentence for murder, Kojo was back on the street a month after Johnny Boy. After only being gone for four months, Kojo was able to pick up where he left off, only now he had a quality product and muscle behind him. With the Curcio family's boss, the late Big Tony Collette, wanting a greater presence in the market, he saw Kojo as an opportunity. But one thing stood in his way: the Caldwell Enterprise.

NYPD Deputy Inspector Cavanaugh and Assistant United States Attorney Dennis Allen, who each had been in Big Tony's pocket for years, organized a task force, headed by Lieutenant Rachael Dawkins, to move the Caldwell Enterprise out of their way.

That effort got a big boost when Detectives Bautista and Dickerson dropped Hugo Peterson, aka Pistol Pete, in Lieutenant Dawkins's lap. He had witnessed Gavin Caldwell and two women killing Greg Mac.

"One had on white leather pants and a floor-length coat, a blond wig, and big glasses. The other one had on a red floor-length leather coat and some tight-ass red booty shorts. And both of them were wearing bulletproof vests," Pistol had told Lieutenant Dawkins, who had no idea that the women were Rain Robinson and Jackie Washington.

Rain found out about it because a member of Barbara's crew, Jolina Booker, had been working task force detective Darius Hudson for information. She overheard him talking about it and called Barbara. She immediately called her captain. Once Jackie told Rain, she knew what she had to do to avoid The Family being dragged into their investigation: kill everybody who could place Rain and Jackie in that room.

Between the work of the task force and the engagement of The Family, the Caldwell Enterprise was dealt a blow that Butch Caldwell, who ran the operation from his prison cell, knew he couldn't come back from. When the investigation came too close to Gavin and his sister, London, the decision was made to get out of the New York market and move his family's business to Arizona. The first to go was Fredricka. She moved after she killed her husband when he became a task force informant. When the second of London's girlfriends became a task force informant, London had her killed, and then she moved to Arizona as well. Gavin hung around long enough to oversee the move of the family's financial service company, Anderson Montgomery, before he was gone too.

With its mission accomplished, and Angelo Collette now being boss of the Curcio family, Deputy Inspector Cavanaugh and Assistant United States Attorney Dennis Allen congratulated Lieutenant Dawkins on a job well done. She told them that although she was winding down the Caldwell investigation, she was turning her attention to Kordell Jones, who was positioning himself to fill the void left by the Caldwells. She knew that there was something funny going on when the lieutenant was informed that her task force was being integrated into the organized crime task force's investigation of Rocco Vinatieri.

Therefore, Dawkins didn't tell them that she had already placed a deep-cover operative inside Kojo's organization. Her name was Veronica Isley. After serving two tours in Afghanistan, she joined the police force. Isley graduated in the top five at the police academy and was recruited by Dawkins for the assignment. After Isley acknowledged the risk, Dawkins decided not to bring her in. So now Isley was out there on her own with no support.

Since Johnny Boy brought Kojo into the business, Black had assumed that he ran a tight program. Jackie had Marvin and Baby Chris on it, but Carter thought that, in his position, he needed to be on top of it as well, especially since Ryder, the acting captain of his crew, and Truck, one of Kojo's dealers, had a personal beef. Carter wanted to talk to Rain about it, but she wasn't taking his calls.

He was the underboss of the family, so if anything came of it, he would handle the situation without her. That was what Black put him in that spot for: to step up and handle shit when Rain didn't. He thought back to the day when Black invited him to Freeport.

"I want you to take Howard Owens's place as captain of his crew."

Carter had just gotten out of prison and was thinking about going legit and spending the rest of his life with Mileena. He knew that he had come to Freeport for Black to convince him to get back in. But Carter never expected Black to offer him the captain's chair.

"You're the only one I can trust."

Carter accepted that responsibility. That was why he was there: his loyalty and dedication to Mike Black. It was that dedication that made him choose The Family over Mileena time after time until she had enough and walked away. Then Black asked him to be Rain's consigliere. When he said yes, Carter understood that his role was to be a stabilizing influence for the young boss of The Family, but more importantly, that his role was to protect Black's interest. That was why he was there.

With that newfound sense of clarity, Carter said, "Fuck her," and drove to his spot, Romans, the pizzeria and sports-betting spot that Carter once again operated from. He had been running his crew out of the second office at J.R.'s, but once he and Rain started fucking, that was all they did when they were there. So he made the move back to Romans because he felt like she was blowing his mind with that insane pussy Rain was slinging. He thought for a while that was the reason she cut him off, but it wasn't. All that did was give them another place to fuck.

As it always was when Carter walked into Romans, everybody wanted to shake hands or bump fists with the underboss of The Family. Some people wanted to talk to Carter about their issues, while others needed a favor. Some people at Romans just spoke so others would see them and know that Carter knew their name. However it went, it usually took about twenty minutes before he got to his office and was able to shut the door.

He sat down at his desk. It was in that room, on that desk, that it happened. Those days, he and Rain were hot for each other. They couldn't get enough of the other, and any time alone was an opportunity to fuck some more. Her sex was incredible. Although Carter hated to admit it, Rain had pussy whipped his ass, and then she unceremoniously dumped him.

"But why? That's what I can't figure out. Why?" Carter said aloud. "Everything was going fine until . . ." Carter paused as enlightenment finally broke through. "Until Miranda."

Although it was enlightening, it confused him even more.

"Having a threesome was her idea. It was what she wanted to do."

After a shootout to cover their involvement in Greg Mac's assassination, Rain was looking around at the carnage they'd caused and found herself in heat and wanting not only Carter but Jackie as well. Her mind had begun to wander.

I bet Jackie sucks the fuck out some pussy, Rain thought. But she quickly dismissed the idea because fucking both of her captains was a really bad idea.

Carter remembered being reluctant when Rain first suggested it to him. His first thought was that it was some type of girlie trap that he needed to be careful not to fall into as he had with Mileena. When she brought up the idea of them having a threesome with Yarrisa, Carter got excited about the idea because he had wanted to fuck Yarrisa for a while. Then Mileena flipped it on him. He could hear her angrily shouting, "Oh, so you do want to fuck Yarrisa!" It was a trap, and his falling into it was a big mistake. And Carter always tried to learn from his mistakes and never make them again.

But then he thought about it. If Rain Robinson said that she wanted to have a threesome, then Rain Robinson wanted to have a threesome, so he was down for it. They went to a club called Hang Ups, and Rain picked Miranda herself. And once Rain had firmly established, "I don't eat pussy," to which Miranda replied, "I do," she looked at Carter. "And I love to suck dick."

They left Hang Ups and headed for the hotel. Now Rain was barely speaking to him, but Miranda called damn near every day. The thought frustrated him, and he picked up the phone to call her again.

What happened to fuck her?

When the phone began ringing again, Rain picked it up and once again sent the call to voicemail. Since she found her cousin, Sapphire, safe and unharmed, they had been hiding out at Wanda's safe house, and they were there for two reasons. Not only was her safe house better fortified and better stocked than Rain's, but Carter had no idea where it was, so he couldn't just show up when he felt like it.

They were hiding at Wanda's safe house because somebody was trying to kill Sapphire. When Rain went looking for Sapphire at her apartment, a man had ransacked the place, and she had to fight him off. Until Rain could figure out who was trying to kill her and why, they were staying put.

The phone rang again, and Rain was about to send the call to voicemail.

"Why don't you just answer it?" Sapphire asked because she was tired of hearing it ring.

"Because I don't feel like being bothered with him."

"Then tell him to fuck off and kiss your natural black ass. That's what I always do."

Rain laughed, and then she swiped to talk. "What do you want?"

"Really?" Her attitude frustrated him. "Where are you?"

"I'm fine."

"That's not what I asked you."

"But that's what I'm telling you."

"When are you going to stop this shit and talk to me?"

"When are you going to stop fuckin' around and tell me about Fantasy?"

There was silence on the line.

"That's what I thought," Rain said and ended the call.

"Baby daddy?" Sapphire asked.

"Yeah."

"I know you didn't ask me, but you know what I think," Sapphire said as her phone began to ring.

"Saved by the bell."

"I heard that, cuz," Sapphire said, looking at the display. Seeing that it was her mother, she swiped to talk. "Hi, Mommy."

"Not Mommy," a male voice said.

"Who is this?"

"If you want to see your mother alive again, bring the drive to her house."

"What drive?"

"Bring the drive to her house now or your mother dies. And come alone."

"What drive?" Sapphire shouted, but he had ended the call.

"Who was that?" Rain asked.

"I don't know, but whoever it was is at Mommy's house, and he said he'll kill her if I don't bring the drive."

"What drive?"

"I don't know," Sapphire said, and then she thought about it. "Wait a second." She rushed out of the room.

"What?" Rain said and got up to follow her to the room she was staying in.

"I remember finding a drive on the last flight I worked." Sapphire put her suitcase on the bed and opened it. "I thought that I turned it in but"—she paused as she riffled through the suitcase, looking for her uniform—"I guess I didn't." Sapphire pulled the drive out of the pocket.

"Whatever is on that drive, people are willing to kill for it."

"What am I gonna do?" Sapphire asked and plopped down on the bed.

"We're gonna save your mother, that's what we're going to do. Come on," Rain said and went to get her guns and put on her vest. "Call Carla, Alwan. Tell her to meet me at her office. I got some shit I need her to do."

When they arrived at the office, not only was Carla there, but Monika was there as well. When Rain's aunt Priscilla first came to her about finding Sapphire, she had Carla investigate the place where Rain was told Sapphire worked, Overseas Air. At the time, she couldn't find out much about them because they didn't have much of a digital footprint, but she promised to stay on it and dig deeper. She was eventually able to tell Rain that Overseas Air was a front company for an Albanian mafia organization called the Troka Clan, but not until after Rain had burned the place to the ground. The Clan was engaged in the international trafficking of human organs, tissues, and other body products. Therefore, when she got the call from Alwan to meet Rain in the office at that hour, Carla thought that calling Monika, who was highly skilled in weapons and commando tactics, was a good idea.

"I need you to copy whatever is on this drive," Rain ordered, handing the drive to Carla. "Then I need you to find out what the fuck is on there that's worth killing over."

"I'm on it," Carla said and got to work.

"What's going on, sunshine?" Monika asked.

"People who want that drive are holding her mother." Rain pointed at Sapphire, and then she paused. "Oh, yeah, this is my cousin, Sapphire. That's Monika and that's Carla."

"Hi." Sapphire waved.

"Got it," Carla said when she finished copying the data and handed the drive back to Rain.

"Thanks."

"What are you going to do now?" Monika asked.

"I'm going to trade this drive for her mother." Rain started for the door.

"Who you got with you?" Monika asked, walking alongside her.

"Alwan is with me."

"Stop!"

Rain stopped. "What?"

"You're going to fuck with the Albanian mob? Just you and Alwan?" She shook her head. "I'm coming with you.

You too, Carla," Monika said, walking away. "Give me a second to gear up."

"Hurry up," Rain said, thinking that she had no idea what she was walking into. Bringing Monika along was a smart idea.

Once Monika was ready, they left the office and headed for Aunt Priscilla's house. The plan was for Alwan and Rain to drive Sapphire to the house, while Monika and Carla followed in the security van. They wouldn't be able to have eyes inside the house, but with the equipment in the van, they would at least know how many people were in the house and where they were from their heat signatures.

"I don't like it, sunshine. Sending her in there alone is a bad idea," Monika said when they got to the house.

"I don't like it either. But if we rush the house, they will kill my aunt. You got a better idea, now's the time to tell me."

"I didn't know you had any family other than Miles," Monika said since she didn't have a better idea.

"My mother's people."

"All right, we do it their way." She turned to Carla. "How many people are in there?"

"Three. Two in the front of the house and another at the back door."

"Okay," Monika began. "I'll take the back." Monika exited the van and started to walk away, but then she stopped. "We killing these fucks, or we letting them walk away with what they came for?"

Rain paused to think. "We'll see how it goes. Go ahead, Sapphire. I'll be right outside," she said, and then she started for the house.

She let Sapphire get a little ahead of her, and then Rain started for the house behind her. Sapphire was scared as she walked to the house, but she was more scared of what they had done or might do to her mother. She opened the gate and walked to the door, surprised at how calm she was.

The people who are trying to kill you are holding Mommy, and you're walking up here like you don't have a care in the world, Sapphire thought. She was running on pure adrenaline as she got to the door.

Since she had one, she thought for a second about using her key, but that might get her or her mother shot. So Sapphire rang the bell and waited.

"I'm in position and standing by, sunshine," Monika said over coms.

"Acknowledged. I'm out front," Rain said. "The door just opened, and she went in."

"Standing by."

As soon as Sapphire was inside, the man slammed the door and put a gun to her head. "Did you bring it?"

"Yes, I have it."

He grabbed her by the arm and walked her into the living room at gunpoint. As she came into the room, she saw her mother. She was standing in the middle of the room, gagged, hands zip-tied, and a gun to her head.

"Are you all right, Mommy?" Sapphire asked.

Her mother nodded her head.

The man hit Sapphire in the back of the head. "Of course she is all right. We are not animals."

"Fuck that," the man holding Aunt Priscilla said and pressed the barrel against her head. "Where is the drive?"

"In my pocket."

"Reach for it slowly and toss it on the floor near me."

With a gun still pointed at her head, Sapphire reached slowly into her pocket, pulled out the drive, and tossed it on the floor. When she did, the man holding her pushed her to the floor and picked up the drive.

"Thank you," the other man said and shot Aunt Priscilla.

"Mommy!" Sapphire screamed as she fell to the ground.

He turned his weapon on Sapphire and was about to shoot her when Rain kicked in the front door and Monika came in the back door firing.

Rain's first shot hit the man with the gun on Sapphire in the arm, and he dropped the gun right before Monika shot him in the back of the head. The other man fired a couple of shots at Rain, and he ran out the front door. As soon as he hit the porch, Alwan put three in his chest.

Chapter Five

Detectives Jack Harmon and Diane Mitchell had been investigating the murders of Elias Colton and Quentin Hunter. Their primary suspect, Daniel Beason, had disappeared without a trace, as had Andrea Frazier, the chief operating officer of his bank, Rockville Guaranty Savings and Loan. The two were last seen leaving their office in Frazier's BMW on the day Hunter was murdered.

In the days since, the investigation had gone cold, and the detectives caught another case: the murder of Oliva Deacon. She had been reported missing three months ago by her daughter. The missing person case became an active murder investigation when a set of dentures and the partial remains of a foot were found in the sewer by a city worker. After a forensic dental analysis, a positive identification was made using a discreet identification code that was embedded in the denture base.

The investigation quickly led to George McSwain, who had sold Deacon fraudulent stock shares from the estates of his deceased clients at below-market rates. When she became suspicious of the scheme, McSwain feigned interest in a house that she was selling and lured her to his home office. He shot Deacon in the head and then put her body in a forty-gallon drum of concentrated sulfuric acid. Two days later, McSwain found that Deacon's body had mostly dissolved, and thinking that if there was no body, there was no crime, he emptied the drum into a sewer, confident that he had gotten away with murder.

That morning, Jack and Diane were on their way to McSwain's house to arrest him for her murder, but he wasn't at home.

"So what do you wanna do now?" Diane asked as they walked away from the door.

"We could check out the phony office again," Jack offered.

"That was a waste of time the first two times we went there," Diane said as they got to the car.

"Maybe the third time is the charm. I don't know."

She leaned on the car. "Or we could take another run at Susan," Diane suggested. She was the wife of their primary suspect, Daniel Beason.

"You think he reached out to her?"

"He might have. You never know. What else do we have to do?" Diane smiled as they got in the car.

"Nothing."

"And you know you wanna see what Susan wears for you today."

Jack started the car and drove away. "She does not dress for me."

"Yes, she does. Unless she prances around the house with her hair and makeup done, dressed like she just walked off the cover of a magazine, she dresses for you, Jack."

"Maybe she dresses for you."

"Right." Diane laughed. "It's true, women do dress to impress and outdress each other, but look at how I'm dressed. Dark blue suit, white blouse, and flat shoes."

Jack chuckled. "You dress like a cop."

"In case you forgot, I am a cop."

"I noticed, being your partner and all."

"In every sense of the word."

"Okay," Jack conceded, "maybe she does get dressed up when we get there, but I'm more interested in knowing if he reached out to her or if she remembered something we could use."

"I bet she wears something that shows off her abs and the belly ring." She giggled. "Since you stare at it."

"I do not stare at her belly ring or her amazing abs," Jack laughed, and Diane nodded her head.

"See?" She laughed. "She knows you like it, so she shows it off for you. The woman craves male attention. After being married to a man who ignored her for as long as she claims Beason did, she needs to feel attractive and desirable to men."

"So what are you saying, that I should cater to that need?"

"If it gets us information, by all means. Just don't cross the line."

"Noted, don't cross the line, but I honestly don't think she knows much more than she's told us. Remember she told you that she wasn't his partner."

"She was his property, I remember," Diane said sadly, remembering how she felt when Susan first told her that. Property or not, Diane believed that Susan was holding something back.

When they arrived at Susan's house, she surprised the detectives by answering the door herself. Since Beason had come under suspicion of murder, her mother, sister, and her nephew, Wesley, had been staying at the house with her, and it was usually Wesley who answered the door. That day, Susan was wearing a red pleated tent minidress with red embellished satin wraparound high-heel sandals, and much to Diane's surprise, she wasn't showing off her abs.

Susan smiled when she saw Jack. "Good morning, Detective Harmon," she sang, and Diane rolled her eyes.

"Sorry to keep showing up like this and bothering you, Mrs. Beason," Jack began.

"No bother at all," Susan said, stepping aside to let them in. She was getting tired of them just showing up. "But I only have a few minutes. I was just on my way out."

Diane leaned close to Jack. "That explains it," she whispered.

"Behave."

"And before you ask," Susan said, leading them into the living room, "I haven't heard anything from Danny." She lied easily. She sat down, crossed her legs, and Jack got an eyeful of her thigh.

"What about Andrea Frazier? Have you heard anything from her?" Diane asked, and Susan looked at the detective as if she had spit in her face.

"No," she said angrily. "And why would I have heard from any of Danny's whores?"

Jack and Diane looked at one another. "Was your husband involved with Ms. Frazier on something other than a professional level, Mrs. Beason?" he asked, attempting to be delicate because Diane had struck a nerve.

Susan smiled warmly at Jack. "I don't know that for sure, but I accepted his relationships with his senior female staff a long time ago, Detective Harmon. I imagine Andrea was no different from the rest."

"I understand."

"Do you know anything about Quentin Hunter's murder and if it relates to the Colton murder?" Diane asked.

Susan looked sternly at Diane. "I'm going to tell you this again, Detective Mitchell. I have no idea what Danny was engaged in, where he might be hiding, or how it relates to Quentin's and Elias's murders. I honestly don't want to know, and I honestly don't care. I'm sure by now he's out of the country."

"Thank you very much, Mrs. Beason. We appreciate your time," Diane said and stood up.

Susan stood up, looking annoyed at Diane. "Yes. I'm sure you do."

"Sorry to have bothered you," Jack said.

Susan smiled. "No bother at all, Detective Harmon. I'm happy to cooperate in any way that I can," she said and led them to the door. When she opened the door, Susan smiled again. "See you in a couple of days," she said, waving as the detectives walked to their car.

Once they were in the car, Jack looked at Diane. "Okay, I see what you mean."

"She was damn near hostile to me. But you . . ." Diane said, laughing as Jack drove away. "'No bother at all, Detective Harmon. See you in a couple of days.' Pathetic."

"Where you wanna go now?" he asked to get Diane back on task.

"Since we're following up today, I say we roll by Executive Flight Lines. I'm thinking that it's been a couple of days. Maybe he went back and caught a flight out of the country."

When Jack and Diane got to Executive Flight Lines, they found that the small private airline was under new management. The previous manager had been extremely helpful and had willingly provided the detectives with all the information they asked for. Her cooperation with the police in the delicate investigation had cost the young manager her job. Therefore, when Jack and Diane asked the new manager if Beason had booked a flight in the last seven days, he advised the detectives that Executive Flight Lines would no longer provide any information on their clients without a warrant.

"You do understand that this is a murder investigation. Two men are dead, and a woman is missing," Jack said.

"Yes, Detective Harmon, I am fully aware of the situation, and although I am sympathetic to your request, I can't release any information to you without a warrant."

"Fine." Diane pointed in his face. "You need a warrant?" She took out her phone. "You got one."

"Who are you calling?" the manager asked.

"I'm calling Judge Peterson to expedite a warrant. And then I'm gonna go wait outside and introduce myself to all your clients as they come in. You know, the ones whose privacy you're trying so hard to protect. I'm going to tell them that I'm waiting here for Judge Peterson to approve my expedited warrant request for their personal information."

"What do you think your clients will do when word gets around?" Jack asked.

"And believe me, I will make it my mission in life to make sure word gets around." Diane leaned over the counter and stared directly into his eyes. "Because I'm a cop, and I don't have shit else to do all day but find new and creative ways to fuck with you until I get what I want."

The manager quickly turned to his monitor, tapped a couple of keys, and a few quick clicks later, he said, "He hasn't boarded a flight since he returned from his trip to Paris."

"Was that so hard?" Jack asked and turned to leave.

Diane smiled. "Thank you for your time and cooperation. You've been immensely helpful."

And with that, Jack and Diane left Executive Flight Lines. "I love it when you play bad cop," Jack said on the way to the car.

Diane stopped and looked Jack in the eyes. "Whoever said I was playing?" She paused. "It's just that nobody ever tries me."

"Remind me to stay on your good side." He held the door open for Diane, and she got in the car.

"What now?" Diane asked when Jack got in.

"Let's see if George McSwain is home," he said and drove that way.

When they got to McSwain's house, the detectives approached with weapons drawn. Jack knocked on the door and identified himself. "NYPD!"

The suspect began firing at them through the door.

Diane got on the radio. "I have shots fired at this location!" she said as Jack kicked in the door and went in. "Requesting backup!"

When Diane entered the house, a man she'd never seen before fired at her. She dove for the floor and crawled behind the couch. She looked for Jack. He was exchanging gunfire with McSwain. The shooter fired at Diane and then ducked into the hallway. She got to her feet and started down the hall after him, but she didn't see him.

"Jack!" she yelled when she heard shots being fired in another part of the house.

Then she heard footsteps. Diane turned in time to see a door open. The man appeared, and he shot at her. She returned fire and hit him with two shots in his chest. Diane walked up to him and kicked his gun away.

She reloaded her weapon. "Jack!" she yelled once she had cleared the hall.

"He's going out the back!" Jack yelled, and Diane ran toward the back door.

McSwain tried to make it out the back door, firing shots blindly at Jack. When Diane heard footsteps coming toward her, she raised her weapon and set herself. When McSwain ran out, she was waiting.

"Freeze!" she shouted and took aim.

When McSwain raised his gun, Diane fired and hit him in the chest. The impact of the shot took him off his feet. Jack kicked the gun away.

"You good?"

"Yeah, I'm good."

Chapter Six

It was late in the evening when the charter plane carrying Daniel Beason landed at Sky Acres Airport, a public-use airport located six miles southwest of the central business district of Millbrook, a city that was ninety miles north of New York City. Knowing that he was a suspect in two murders, he decided that it was best not to arrive in the city from Turks and Caicos.

In the 1970s, the Turks and Caicos Islands were declared an official offshore center. That meant there were no taxes on income or capital gains, no inheritance or estate taxes, and there were strict confidentiality laws. The Turks and Caicos Islands provided a full range of international banking and trust services. As there was no direct taxation, Turks and Caicos banks were able to offer their clients higher rates of return and lower margin costs, making it an attractive location for people trying to hide their money.

Beason had come there looking for the information that Elias Colton had gotten from the Albanians. He had become involved with Elvana Vetone, the daughter of Troka Clan member Saemira Vetone, and he convinced her to give him the data. It was Elvana who snuck into her father's house and copied data on transactions, dates, times, contacts, and their locations. Colton thought that being in possession of the information would put him and Beason in a stronger position, but it just ended up getting him killed.

After Lendina Neziri, the Mik of the Troka Clan, killed Andrea Frazier and left Beason alone in the warehouse, he looked at her body and the blood pooling around her head.

"Sorry, Andrea."

He stooped down and picked up her purse, quickly got her phone and the $20,000 he had given her, and he left the warehouse on foot. Once he had gotten somewhere he thought he'd be safe for a while, he got Andrea's phone and called the last number she dialed.

As he expected, her last call was to her pilot friend. Once Beason explained the situation and that Andrea was dead, the pilot agreed to take him to the island. But instead of the $15,000 he'd told Andrea it would cost to take him there, now the pilot wanted $25,000 in cash and upfront.

"Or the wheels never leave the tarmac."

"Deal," Beason said, wondering where he was going to get the other $5,000 he would need.

He had to chuckle because, at times like this, he would call Quentin, and he would have given him the money. But he was dead. Quentin was the first person he met when his parents dropped him off at college. They became fast friends and, eventually, roommates. Now he was dead, and Beason knew that he was responsible.

What was Quentin doing there? he'd asked himself a thousand times. But Beason had to set his grief aside for the moment and figure out where he was going to get the money, and at the same time, he knew that he only really had one choice. It was risky, but it was a risk that he had to take.

"You got a lot of nerve calling me," Susan's sister said.

"I know, and I'm sorry to drag you into this, but I need you to get a message to Susan."

"Haven't you caused her enough harm?"

He really didn't have time for this. "Yes, I have, and I'm trying to fix it, but I need her help."

Beason told her that he had $10,000 in their home safe, and arrangements were made for her son, Wesley, to deliver the money. When Beason arrived in Turks and Caicos, he asked the pilot to come back for him in a couple of days, but he refused.

"I can pay you double," Beason said because he had money in several banks on the island.

"I really don't give a fuck. Andrea was good people. Now get the fuck off my plane."

It didn't matter. He was there, and Beason would find a way back once he had gotten what he came for. The thing to do then was to make his way to Colton's house in the Cooper Jack Bay settlement. He caught a cab to the house, and when he arrived, Beason went around to the back of the house. He jimmied the lock and went in. The place looked different somehow, but he attributed that to the fact that he hadn't been in the house in years. Beason looked around and wondered where to begin his search.

"Don't move," a female voice said and cocked the hammer on her gun. Beason put his hands up. "Turn around, slowly. I don't mind shooting you," she said, and he did as he was told.

"Marva?" Beason said to the woman with the thick salt-and-pepper dreadlocks pointing a gun at his head.

"Danny?"

"What are you doing here?"

"I live here. What are you doing here?"

"Elias is dead."

"I know. That doesn't answer my question though. What are you doing in my house?"

"I think that Elias may have left some important information here. I came to see if I can find it."

"Is that what got him killed?"

"Yes."

"It got him killed, and now you're looking for it?"

"Or they'll kill me too." He paused. "Can I put my hands down now, Marva?"

She lowered the gun and nodded. "Go ahead."

"Thank you. Can I sit?"

"Go ahead, have a seat," Marva said, and she sat down too, but she kept the gun in her hand.

"Wow, Marva. What's it been, fifteen years?"

"Seventeen. I've been down here for seventeen years." It was seventeen years ago that Marva Nichols gave Elias Colton an ultimatum.

"You can be with me, or you can be with Cissy, but not both." After sharing her bed with him for the last five years, Marva had reached her breaking point. It broke her heart when he told her that he was staying with Cissy.

Staying with Cissy's money was closer to the truth. Divorcing Cissy would ruin him, his company, and everything he had spent a lifetime building, he explained to her. "I love you, Marva, and I always will, but I can't lose everything," he told her, and that made the hurt even greater. He had chosen money and power over being with her.

So she left. Without letting him know where she was going or saying goodbye, Marva left the country. She had some money in the First Caribbean International Bank on the island. Her plan was to cash out and decide what to do from there. She had been there for a week when she opened her hotel room door, and Colton was standing there. Marva let him in, and she made it clear to him that their relationship was over and there was nothing that he could say or do that would change her mind. Colton said that he understood, but he still wanted to take care of her, so he bought her that house and put it in Marva's name so Cissy would never find it.

"As many times as I've been here, I never knew you lived here."

Marva chuckled. "I was right here in the house every time you were here."

"I did not know that."

"How would you? You always insisted on staying in a hotel when you were on the island."

"That's true."

"So what information are you looking for?" Marva asked, and once Beason explained with as little information as he could, Marva suggested that he should get started with Colton's computer. She showed him the way to the room that Colton stayed in when he came to the island.

"Over means over. At least it does to me," Marva said.

"I see," Beason said and got started.

It didn't take long for him to realize that the files he needed weren't on that computer. Therefore, with Marva's permission and assistance, they began searching the house. It was almost midnight when Beason put his hands up in surrender. Marva had given up an hour before that and was sitting outside on the lanai, sipping a cocktail, when Beason came and sat down next to her.

"Any luck finding it?"

"Nothing."

"I can't think of anyplace else to tell you to look."

"It's not here. I was sure that if he kept a copy, it would be here."

"The only other thing I can think to tell you is that Elias had a safe deposit box at CIBC First Caribbean Bank. Maybe it's in there. I have a banking relationship with the bank's manager. We can go by there tomorrow morning, and I'll see what I can do. Other than that, I can't help you."

"Thank you, Marva. You've done more than enough."

"In the meantime, I'm going to call it a night. Do you have someplace to stay on the island?" she asked since he usually stayed in a hotel.

"No. I came straight here from the airport."

"You're welcome to stay if you like."

"I wouldn't want to put you out."

Marva stood up. "You are not putting me out. Come on. I'll show you to your room, and we can go to the bank first thing in the morning."

After a long and refreshing hot shower, Beason got into bed and tried to get some rest, but he found himself thinking about the mess he was in. The information that was contained on the drive wasn't there. What he had to think about was what he was going to do if Marva came up empty at the bank the following day. What was he going to do next? Stay in Turks and Caicos, or go somewhere else and start over? He didn't know, but Beason decided that he would make that decision after they went to the bank.

However, the following morning when they arrived at CIBC First Caribbean Bank to see if Marva could talk the manager into allowing them to look at Colton's safe deposit box, things fell apart seconds after they walked through the door.

Marva looked around for her contact. "I don't see him," she said.

Beason looked around the bank, covered his face, and turned around quickly.

"We have to get out of here now."

"Why? What's wrong?"

"Meagan is here."

"Meagan Colton?"

Beason nodded.

"Where?" Marva asked anxiously.

"At the desk with the blonde in the blue dress," Beason said, pointing in that direction as discreetly as he could.

Marva looked at the young woman she had known since she was a baby. When Meagan was very young, Marva was Daddy's little secret whom Mommy could never know about. She smiled as they left the bank, thinking that the price of young Meagan's silence was ice cream and watching the cartoons that her mother wouldn't allow her to see.

Dejected, Beason walked away from the bank knowing that if the information was in that safe deposit box, it was unavailable to him now. As they drove back to Marva's house, Beason knew that it was decision time. He had some money in several of the banks on the island, so he would be all right. The bulk of his money was stashed in banks in Switzerland, but since Neziri's associate, Besnike Fazliu, was in Switzerland, that was the last place he wanted to go.

You need to go back and clear your name, he thought.

Beason wondered, if the information were in the safe deposit box, would Cissy, not knowing what it was, turn it over to the police? Then it occurred to him that if Meagan was now in possession of the information, she may be in danger too.

All the more reason to go back and clear your name.

He was accused of murdering his two best friends, something that he could never do. Although he had his suspicions, Beason had no idea who killed Quentin, but he knew that Neziri killed Colton and Andrea Frazier. He was a witness to both murders. That meant that all he had to do was go to the police and tell them what really happened. Of course, he would have to tell the police everything that he and Colton were involved in, but at least he wouldn't have to spend the rest of his life on the run.

No, you'd be in jail. He laughed aloud.

"What?" Marva asked.

"Just thinking about the reality of my situation," Beason said, because the truth was, even if he did go to the police and tell them everything and they by chance believed him, and they arrested Neziri for the murder, and by some miracle he avoided going to prison, he would still have the rest of the Troka Clan to deal with.

"And that is?" Marva asked as she pulled into her driveway.

"That I need to go back. There is no way in hell that Elias didn't make a copy of the data. I just need to find where that is and return it to them." He chuckled. "Then I need to convince the police that I didn't kill my two best friends, without implicating the guy who actually did it."

"Good luck with that," she said and got out of the car. Beason followed her inside the house.

"Thanks. How I'm gonna do all that, I have no idea," he said, chuckling as he closed the door behind them.

"Neither do I," Marva said, and then she stopped moving and held up one finger.

"What?"

"Somebody is in here," she said, noticing that one of her couch pillows was in the wrong place.

Just then, a man came rushing out of the coat closet and tackled Beason. As they wrestled around on the floor, Marva got her gun. With one in the chamber, she took aim as the men rolled around on the floor, exchanging blows until the intruder got on top of Beason and began choking him.

Beason heard the shot.

And then he saw the shock in his adversary's eyes, then watched the life disappear from him. The grip around his throat loosened before he fell to the floor.

"Thank you," Beason said, trying to catch his breath. He got to his feet.

"You're welcome. Now you need to get out of here," Marva said, waving the gun toward the door.

"Thank you, Marva," Beason said and left her to deal with the police.

Beason made his way to the banks he had on the island and closed his accounts. Now that he had money, Beason had to ask himself again, *do I want to go back or start over?* If he decided to start over, that meant he was going to Switzerland and would take his chances with Besnike Fazliu because there was no way he could start over with the money he had.

"Where to?" the driver asked when Beason got in a cab after leaving the bank.

"Just drive and I'll let you know."

As he sat looking out the window, Beason thought about Quentin and Andrea, Susan, and now Marva. Two of them were dead because of him, and there was no telling what was going to happen to Marva when the police came. And Susan would be left to clean up the mess from the Rousseau Land Development scheme that he and Colton ran to funnel millions of dollars through several front companies and intermediaries to finance their smuggling operation. Each of their sacrifices demanded that he go back and find a way to make this right.

So he was back in the country, ninety miles away from the city, not really knowing what he was going to do but determined to do it.

Chapter Seven

"You got a body!" were the very first words that Jack and Diane heard the second they walked into their unit.

An hour later, they were walking into a warehouse on Columbia Street in the Red Hook section of Brooklyn. When responding to reports of a foul odor coming from a vacant warehouse, officers found the decomposing body of Andrea Frazier.

"I guess she didn't run off with Beason," Diane said, putting on her gloves as they entered the warehouse.

"Detectives Harmon and Mitchell," Jack said, introducing themselves to the officer in charge of the scene.

"They tell me this one's yours." He gladly turned to the body. "Based on the rate of decomposition, I'd say she's been here between three and five days."

"That tracks with them leaving the bank in Andrea's car," Jack said.

"Our witness could only say that he saw them leaving the building together. We only assumed they were running away together because her car was gone and his car was still there."

"So are we assuming that Beason killed her?" Jack asked.

"Only because he was the last one she was seen with. But we can't rule out that Beason left the bank another way and somebody else killed Frazier."

"And why? Why kill her? What did she know that was worth killing her over?" Jack asked, and Diane didn't say anything for a second or two. "What?"

"I think it's time that we start taking the advice of a killer."

"Who, Black?" Jack asked as the technicians took Andrea Frazier's body away.

"Yeah. It's deeper than that. That's what he said, that Albert and Gayle look good for it, but it's deeper than that." Diane started walking. "I think we've been looking at this thing all wrong from the beginning."

He walked alongside her. "I don't follow you."

"At first, we were sure—at least, I was sure—that Albert killed Colton because he was fucking his wife."

"Your usual."

Diane believed that most if not all murders fell into two categories, sex or money, and she was usually proven right. On the surface, the Colton case appeared to have both.

"Right. But at every turn, we've been proven wrong and have had to reevaluate our theory of the crime." Jack chuckled. "We've reevaluated it so often that we don't have a working theory of the crime at this point."

"Because we're not looking at the bigger picture."

"Which is?"

Diane stopped. "Shit, Jack, if I knew that, we'd have somebody in handcuffs by now."

"Okay, so let's start at the beginning. Think big picture." Jack started toward the exit. "Why was Elias Colton murdered? What do Quentin Hunter and Andrea Frazier have to do with it?"

"Honestly, Jack, I'm just not buying that all these murders are to cover up some fraud scheme." She shook her head. "Something triggers Beason. He goes to Colton's house."

"They fight, and off the balcony he goes."

"But then you murder Frazier and Hunter to cover up some fraud scheme? No, Jack, I'm sorry. It's got to be deeper than that."

Jack laughed. "There's that word again, 'deeper.'"

"So we start with that. Why did he kill Frazier, and why here? Why leave their Manhattan office to kill her in Brooklyn?"

"We know that Colton was in the shipping business."

"And we are near the port," Diane added.

"Let's find out who owns this building," Jack said, and with a new direction to pursue, the detectives left the warehouse.

When Jack and Diane returned to the precinct, they got to work researching who owned the vacant warehouse, which turned out not to be as easy as it should have been. The warehouse was being managed by a small property management company, and the agent Jack spoke to couldn't tell him who actually owned the building. She told the detective that the entire transaction was done via the internet. The company name was listed as Shipping Warehouse. The search took time and went through a sea of LLCs, dummy, and shell companies and ended with a company called Albanian Development. The registered agent was listed as Lule Vata.

"The only other business Albanian Development owns is listed as Tirana," Jack said and noted the address.

"Then that is our next stop," Diane said, and they left the precinct.

When the detectives arrived at Tirana, Diane was surprised that it was a gentlemen's club, but it didn't matter to her. They showed their badges and walked straight to the bar. As the bartender approached, they raised their badges again. When they did, a man who was standing at the bar took off running toward the back of the club.

"I got him," Jack said and ran after him. Diane went out the front door.

Jack chased the man down the hall and out the back door. "Police. Freeze!" Jack shouted and pointed his weapon.

The man turned quickly and opened fire at Jack, and he returned fire. When the man fired back, he ducked around the corner, and Jack went after him. When Jack came around the corner, the man shot at him, and he ducked behind a car. Jack fired again, and the two exchanged fire. He fired two shots and dropped to reload, and the man ran.

"Police!"

The man turned and fired, but his gun was empty. He tossed it in some bushes and kept running. When he rounded the next corner, Diane was there waiting. She holstered her weapon, lowered her shoulder, and ran into the man. They both fell to the ground, but that gave Jack time to catch up.

"Move and I'll kill you," he said with his gun pointed at the man. He looked over at Diane as she got to her feet. "You okay?"

"I'm good," she said, taking out her cuffs. "On your stomach. Hands behind your back."

Once she had him cuffed, Jack jerked him up. "Get up, asshole. You have the right to remain silent and refuse to answer questions. Anything you say may be used against you in a court of law."

When the detectives got him back to the precinct, they found from his driver's license that his name was Ismail Flamur. "And his arrest record is as long as my arm," Santiago said. "Armed robbery, aggravated assault, burglary, grand theft, kidnapping. And those are just the highlights. He's got an open warrant on a burglary charge. For the time being, he's not talking. No English."

"What can you tell us about him, Diego?" Diane asked.

"I can tell you that your boy and the spot you walked up in tonight are Albanian mafia."

What the detective couldn't tell them was that Flamur was the man Rain fought in Sapphire's apartment.

Chapter Eight

Even though it was quiet at the hospital and had been, Monika had Xavier and a five-member security detail on site for protection. Rain was there with Sapphire, and neither one had left the room since Aunt Priscilla got out of surgery. She was going to be fine. The bullet went straight through, and thanks to Monika quickly putting pressure on the wound right away, there wasn't much blood loss. Even though Rain hadn't left the hospital, she was on top of it.

Carter had the entire family out looking for any information they could find about Aunt Priscilla's kidnappers. However, it wasn't until Carla called that Rain got the information she wanted.

"What you got for me, Carla?"

"I think you need to come over here. I don't want to mention any of this over the phone," Carla informed her.

"That bad, huh?"

"It could be. And that is why I think you need to come to the office."

"I'll be there as soon as I can," Rain said and ended the call. "I don't need this shit."

She stood up and looked at Sapphire. She was sitting in the chair next to the bed, holding her mother's hand as she slept. "What's wrong?"

"I gotta head out for a minute, but I'll be back." She glanced at Alwan, and he got up. "I'm gonna leave my people here, so you and Aunt Priscilla will be fine. I promise you that."

"Thanks for everything you've done." Sapphire stood up, and she hugged Rain. "Be careful."

It caught her off guard, as open displays of emotion always did to Rain, but she slowly hugged her cousin back. "I will," Rain said, freeing herself from her cousin's embrace. "Let's go, Alwan."

When Rain and Alwan arrived at the office where Nick ran his security consulting firm, the office was quiet. She went into the operation center, where she could always find Carla, but she wasn't in there.

"Where everybody at?" Rain asked, and Monika came out of her office.

"What's up, sunshine?"

"Carla said she had something that she wanted me to see."

Monika shook her head. "She does. She's in the server room, and she'll be out in a minute."

Rain sat down. "Where's Fantasy? I ain't seen her around lately," she said and looked at Alwan. His eyes got wide at the thought of what Rain might do to her.

"She's on a long-term deep-cover assignment for Wanda. That's all I know," Monika said as Carla came into the room.

Alwan leaned close to Rain. "You're not thinking about killing Fantasy, are you?" he whispered.

Rain glanced at him and smiled. "What you got for me, Carla?"

"I decrypted the drive. It contains information about an Albanian mafia clan. Names, transactions, dates, times, shipping schedules, contacts, payments."

"I'm gonna say that's worth killing for," Monika said.

"What clan?"

"The Troka Clan," Carla said.

"Find out all you can about them and get back to me. I'll be at the hospital," Rain said and left the office to be with her family.

It was a couple of hours later when Monika arrived at the hospital to talk to Rain. She was glad to find that her aunt was awake and in good spirits.

"Got a minute to talk?" Monika asked.

"Be right back," Rain excused herself and went to talk to Monika in the hall.

"What's up?"

"I didn't just meet you, sunshine. So when you said to find out all we could about them, I knew that you meant to find you something you could hit and get back to you."

Rain smiled because Monika was right. "And?" she questioned, wanting to know what she had in mind.

"It's a strip club called Tirana." Monika smiled and put her arm around Rain's shoulder. "You and I haven't rampaged in a long time."

Rain laughed a little. "We haven't, have we?"

"I got your hunting gear in the car. It'll be fun."

"One second," Rain said and stuck her head in the door. "I'll be back, y'all." She turned to the men watching the door. "Nobody gets in. If it ain't me or Monika, they don't get in that room. Understand?"

"Understood."

And with that, Rain left the hospital with Monika. She was quiet on the way out to Tirana, and not hyped about it as Rain usually would be. Monika thought that it was because her aunt was in the hospital, or maybe it was because they were on their way to go fuck with the Albanian mob. Either way, she gave Rain space. And Monika was right, those things were on her mind, but eventually her mind would drift back to being pregnant and her anger at Carter for fucking Fantasy.

"You're not thinking about killing Fantasy, are you?"

Although it was a justifiable question, the answer was no. Rain wasn't thinking about killing Fantasy because she hadn't done anything wrong. And when she really stopped and thought about it, neither had Carter. They were just fucking. Period, end of story. No more need for discussion. And if that were the case, why did it matter to her that Carter fucked Fantasy?

Because I'm pregnant with the nigga's baby, that's why, Rain thought.

"So what's the plan?" Rain asked to escape from the emotional spiral that she was about to enter.

"I know you like to walk in, announce that you are Rain Robinson, and start blasting."

Rain smiled because that was her style.

"And if go-go style is how you wanna do this, you know me, I'm down for that too. But consider this," Monika said and explained what she had in mind. "It may not be as much fun, but I think the big finish at the end makes up for it."

"Definitely not as much fun as firing off a couple of shots and killing anybody who shoots back, but let's do it your way."

When Rain and Monika arrived at Tirana Gentlemen's Club, they exited the vehicle and got to work. Rain looked at the building. "How you planning on getting up there?"

"You just worry about doing what you gotta do and not be seen."

"Yeah, right, like nobody's gonna notice the black woman wandering around the building."

Monika laughed. "It's dark, so maybe they won't notice your black ass, Lorraine."

Rain gave her the finger. "Fuck you, Monika."

"Love you, sunshine. I'll meet you back here in fifteen minutes," Monika said, and they separated to carry out their tasks.

Fifteen minutes later, the ladies were back in the car and ready to get the party started. "Whenever you're ready."

"Do it," Rain said, and Monika pressed engage on her tablet.

Inside Tirana Gentlemen's Club, the men were drinking and the women were dancing and getting paid when an odorless gas laced with oleoresin capsicum, the active ingredient in pepper spray, began emanating from the ventilation system. It didn't take long before the club was filled with smoke. The customers and staff at Tirana experienced an almost instantaneous inflammatory response with intense pain. They began rushing out of the club coughing, choking, and rubbing their eyes.

From their vantage point, Rain and Monika could see the club emptying out. Rain gave them what she considered enough time before she looked at Monika. "Go ahead."

Monika pressed detonate on her tablet, and the first bomb exploded. Since Rain wasn't interested in killing everybody, that small blast was just enough to back the people away from the building. Once they were at a safe distance, Rain gave the order.

"Blow it."

Monika pressed detonate on her tablet, and Tirana Gentlemen's Club exploded. As the fire began to rage out of control, Rain and Monika, who both enjoyed a good explosion, sat in the car and enjoyed the view of the flames lighting up the nighttime sky.

Chapter Nine

He kissed her lips and then her neck, before releasing her breasts from her gown. He ran his tongue down to her cleavage and sucked her delicious nipples. She peeled off her panties and leaned back to enjoy the sensation of his tongue blazing a path down to her navel and then to the wetness between her thighs. He ran his tongue all around her fat, juicy pussy before sucking her clit, and she came hard.

While tremors ran through her body, he thrust himself deep into her. He grabbed her ass, and she wrapped her legs around his waist. He held her legs apart. Her pussy clenched tightly around him as she thrust her ass up off the bed to match each stroke. He stared into her eyes.

"Do you know how much I love you?"

His lips cupped hers, and his tongue attacked hers with fury as they slammed their bodies against each other. She grabbed him and held him tightly as he continued to pummel her. He kissed her again, nibbled her chin, sucked on her neck. She closed her eyes. Feelings of joy and ecstasy were rushing through her body. As the feeling of climax came over her, her eyes sprang open, her breath got caught in her throat, and her mouth opened. She bit her bottom lip to stop herself from screaming and waking up the kids when she felt her body tremble. She clawed at his back and rocked her hips, tossing her body into his, as he pumped harder and felt her juices overflowing.

"Good morning, Mrs. Black."

"Yes, Mr. Black, you are good in the morning."

Once Mr. and Mrs. Black had gotten out of bed and showered, the Black family morning ritual began. While Shy went to see about Mansa, Black went and knocked once on Michelle's door.

"Get up."

And then he went to wake up Easy. Shy took Mansa in the room with her mother so she could get dressed. Downstairs in the kitchen, M, who was always up no later than six, cooked breakfast and got lunch ready for the children.

Since Shy had taken Michelle's car from her for coming in the house at two in the morning after promising her mother that she would be home by ten, William, who usually drove for Black, took Michelle and Easy to school. Therefore, Black had been riding with Shy when Chuck took her to work.

Black had work to do, but he wasn't going to the office that day, so after they dropped Shy off at Prestige Capital and Associates, Chuck dropped Black off at Bobby's house. When he got there, Black and Bobby went to the security consulting firm office. He wanted to go there to see Carla and get her to investigate the Green Ridge Development Corporation and Rousseau Land Development. Even though he thought that Quentin Hunter's death was about more than the land scheme, Black still wanted to know all there was to know.

"And one more thing."

"What's that, Mike?" Carla asked.

"I need you to check out a place called the Tirana Gentlemen's Club. See if they have any ties to the Albanian mob," Black said and saw the look on Carla's face.

"Monika and Rain blew up that place last night," she said sheepishly.

"What?" Black asked.

"Why?" Bobby asked.

Once Carla walked Black and Bobby through everything she knew about Sapphire and the data contained on the drive, she told them that they shot Rain's aunt.

"Which one?" Black asked.

"Priscilla."

"She was fine as hell back in the day," Bobby said.

"Didn't you used to fuck her?"

"Tried to."

"What hospital is she in?"

"Montefiore."

"You tell Monika and Rain that I want to see both of them," he said and left the office with Bobby.

"I'm not liking this already," Bobby said as he drove to the hospital.

"Tell me about it."

"How much do you know about the Albanians?"

"Not much."

"The typical structure of the Albanian mafia is hierarchical, and it's deeply reliant on loyalty, honor, and family, with blood relations and marriage being very important. The clan structure is characterized by strong inner discipline, which is achieved by means of punitive action for any deviation from clan rules. They believe that punishment ensures fear and fear guarantees unconditional loyalty to the clan.

"A clan is led by a Krye. He's the boss, and he selects a Kryetar or an underboss to serve under him. The Kryetar will then choose a Mik, who coordinates the clan's activities. Since Albanian clans are based on blood relations, bonds between them are very strong. The number of clan members are limited by blood relations, making it almost impossible to infiltrate a clan."

"What about the Italian swami?"

Black shook his head. "Angee goes out of his way to steer clear of these guys. Besides, he's got problems of his own. I'll check with Mack, see what the FBI's got on them."

"Yeah, because we need to get on top of this quick." Bobby paused. "I didn't know Rain had any contact with her mother's people."

"Neither did I."

"Not that I blame her. They did shoot her aunt, but she just took us to war."

"I know." Black shook his head. "A couple of days ago, my biggest concern was Michelle worrying me about getting her keys back."

"Which you shouldn't do until she's twenty-one." Bobby laughed. "I still can't believe that you were stupid enough to buy her a car. I just don't see it. What she need with a car?"

"You're starting to sound like Cassandra."

"That's because Shy is smart. Much smarter than you, anyway," Bobby said as they arrived at the hospital. He put the car in park. "You might as well hand her back the keys and crawl back around her little finger where you belong."

"I would, but Cassandra has the keys."

"So you're hiding behind Shy like a little bitch."

"Yup. She asks me about her keys, and I say, 'Go talk to your mother about that.'"

"Smart."

"Thank you," Black said, and they got out of the car and went inside the hospital.

However, when they got to her room, the team Monika had left in place were still guarding the door, and per Rain's instructions, they wouldn't let anybody but her or Monika in the room.

"Do you know who we are?" Bobby asked.

"No, sir, I do not, and I have my orders."

"Why don't you call Monika and ask her if it's all right to let Mike Black and Bobby Ray in this room? Do it now, please, because I don't mind killing you, but you don't want to die," Black said and eased the gun out of his pocket long enough to be seen.

He may not have known who the man was, but he believed that he would kill him, and so he made the call. "She said it's all right."

"Thank you. And you tell her and Rain that I want to see both of them," Black said, and he pushed open the door. When the door opened, both Sapphire and Aunt Priscilla looked up expecting to see Rain, and they were surprised when it wasn't her or Monika.

"Oh, my goodness. Mike Black," Priscilla said when he came through the door. "And Bobby Ray," she said fondly, remembering the days when Bobby used to try to get with her. She was surprised because she hadn't seen either of them in years.

Sapphire's eyes were opened wide in surprise at who her mother knew.

"Hello, Priscilla," Bobby said.

"How are you, Priscilla?" Black asked.

"Other than being shot, I'm fine." She looked at her daughter. "This is my daughter, Sapphire. This is Bobby Ray and Mike Black."

"Nice to meet you, Sapphire," Bobby said.

"I'm glad you're all right," Black said to her.

"Nice to meet both of you." Sapphire looked at her mother. "You and I are going to have a talk about the people you know and didn't tell me about. First, I find out that Rain Robinson is my cousin, and now I find out you know Mike Black and Bobby Ray." She sat down, smiled, and pointed to her mother. "A long talk, Mommy."

Priscilla smiled. "I used to get around before I had you."

"And that is why we are going to talk," Sapphire said, and she laughed, but she was now very curious about the cousin who saved her life and The Family that was now protecting her and her mother.

Once Bobby made Monika's men find two more chairs, he and Black stayed, talking with Priscilla and blowing Sapphire's mind. Although they were having a nice time, Black was hanging around waiting to see if Rain was going to come back there. But after an hour he was ready to go. After saying goodbye to the ladies, Black and Bobby left the hospital. Black wanted to go to see Susan Beason, but Bobby looked at his watch.

"No. You need to go home."

Black looked at the clock on the dashboard. "You're right. Take me home. Susan can wait. We can go see her after dinner."

Now that they were living a more stable life, Black and Shy thought that their family having dinner together every night was important, especially with two teenage children.

"Good, because I'm hungry," Bobby said, and they drove out to New Rochelle for dinner. On the way, Black called FBI Agent Bridgette McCullough.

"I need you to meet me at the Playhouse tonight."

"I'll be there around ten."

Chapter Ten

After delighting with his family in the chicken Alfredo stuffed shells that M had prepared, Black and Bobby left the house and headed back to the city. Everybody always enjoyed it when Bobby came for dinner, and that night was no different, except for Michelle. She made another run at getting the keys to her car back, and she made the mistake of asking her favorite uncle what he thought.

"If it were up to me, your mother would give you back those keys," Bobby said and ate some more chicken Alfredo. "When you graduate from college."

Everybody but Michelle laughed.

"Thank you, Bobby," Shy said happily, looking at her husband.

"Next time you see your cousin Barbara, ask her how old she was when I bought her a car."

"How old was she?" Michelle asked because she thought Barbara was definitely doing it and doing it in style.

"Trick question," Black said to his daughter.

"You never bought her a car, did you?" Michelle asked, looking at the sheer joy in her mother's eyes and knowing that asking her uncle was a bad move.

Black saw it too, so before he left the house, he offered his baby girl some advice. "Stop asking. Every time you do, you see she digs in deeper."

"Yes, Daddy," Michelle said, knowing that the words "when are you gonna give me back my keys" would never cross her lips again. She hugged her father. "Be careful."

"Always."

She let go of Black and looked at Bobby. "Take care of my father."

"Always."

"Traitor." She smiled.

"Just keeping it one hundred," Bobby said and walked out behind Black.

"So you still wanna go talk to Beason's wife?"

"I do."

"What does she look like?"

Black nodded. "Susan is fine as hell. She may be a little heavy chested for your personal taste, but Susan is fine as hell," he repeated.

When they got to the Beason residence, Black and Bobby got out and approached the house. Black rang the bell, and as he usually did, Wesley answered the door.

"Mike Black to see Susan Beason."

"You a cop?"

Bobby looked at him like he was stupid. "Do we look like cops?"

"I'm a friend of the family," Black said calmly.

"Wait a minute," Wesley said and closed the door.

He walked through the living room to the pool where Susan, along with her mother and sister, were hanging out, having drinks, and talking about the position that her husband had left her in.

"Who was at the door, Wesley?" Susan's mother asked.

"Somebody named Mike Black is here to see you, Aunt Susan."

"Oh, shit," Susan said and bounced to her feet.

"What's wrong?" her sister asked.

"Is he another cop?" her mother asked.

Susan answered neither question.

"Wait until I get upstairs to let him in," she said, rushing past Wesley. "Y'all entertain him until I get back," she said to her mother and sister as she went into the house wondering what he was doing there.

Does it matter?

As her mother and sister wondered what was going on, Wesley did what he was told. He let Black and Bobby in and escorted them out to the pool.

"Now I see what the fuss was about," her sister said when she saw Black and Bobby coming.

"Evening, ladies. My name is Mike Black. I'm a friend of Daniel and Susan's."

"Please have a seat. Susan will be back in a minute."

"Thank you. And this is my friend, Bobby Ray."

"Pleasure to meet you ladies," Bobby said as he and Black sat down.

While her mother and sister entertained Black and Bobby at the pool, Susan was in her closet trying to quickly decide what to put on. She had settled on a tan silk cropped top and wide-legged pants, but then she remembered how Black's eyes were drawn to her cleavage the night she wore the Roland Mouret Botez deep V-neck dress to an association meeting.

With that in mind, Susan put on an elegant sleeveless jumpsuit with a deep V neckline that plunged to the wide-belted waist and exaggerated wide-legged pants. She completed the outfit with René Caovilla leather thong sandals and headed downstairs.

"Wesley!" she called to him.

"Yes, Aunt Susan?"

"Go get Mr. Black and bring him in," Susan said, and her nephew did as he was asked.

Susan looked around her living room, thinking of where she wanted to sit to entertain Black. She was a little disappointed when she saw that he wasn't alone, but that didn't matter either. But since he wasn't alone, she decided that she would sit in her Queen Anne chair, and she stood in front of it to receive him.

"Mike Black."

"How are you, Susan?"

"This is unexpected, but a very pleasant surprise," she said and graciously extended her hand toward the couch. "Please, have a seat."

"Thank you, Susan. This is my very good friend, Bobby Ray."

"It is my pleasure to meet you, Mr. Ray."

"Believe me, the pleasure is truly mine." Bobby sat down, thinking, *Black was right. Susan is fine as hell.*

"How have you been holding up during all this, Susan?" Black asked.

"Honestly, Mike, I don't know what to think. I can't believe that Danny would kill Elias or Quentin." Susan paused and looked mournfully at Black. "I didn't get a chance to say how sorry I was for your loss at the funeral." *Because your wife was mean mugging me the entire time.* "I know that you and Quentin were close."

"Thank you, Susan. And that is why I'm here." Black leaned forward. "I don't think that Daniel killed Quentin or Elias either."

"You don't?"

"No, Susan, I don't. So I need you to help me find who did kill Quentin."

Susan smiled excitedly. Before she met and eventually married Beason, Susan was an around-the-way girl from the Bronx. Although she had never met him, Susan knew exactly who Mike Black was the first night that Meka brought him to an Association of Black Businesses meeting and introduced her to him. Titillated by the thought of Mike Black needing her, Susan's smile was almost lecherous.

"Whatever you need from me, Mike, I'm glad to help."

"What were Daniel and Elias involved in?"

"I'm not sure exactly, but I know that they were involved in some type of illegal shipping business with some foreign guys. I heard him and Elias talking about some guy they call Nazzy or something like that."

"Did you hear what they were saying?"

"Danny said that they needed to get out from under this Nazzy guy's thumb."

"What did Quentin have to do with any of that?"

"Nothing." Susan paused. "Elias and Danny had been running some kind of land development scheme for years. They wanted to get Quentin involved with them, but Danny said that he was too much of a Boy Scout to take the risk."

"That sounds like Quentin." Black smiled a little.

Susan inhaled deeply at the sight of it. His smile broadened. So did Susan's.

Bobby shook his head. "How much do you know about the land development scheme?"

"I know they were funneling the money from the development scheme to the shipping business. I can't tell you much more than that." She paused. "The bank is under investigation for the scheme, so I have an appointment to see Connie Lewis in the morning."

"Who's that?"

"She's an FBI investigator." Seeing the concerned look on Black's face, Susan smiled. "Don't worry. In the last couple of weeks, I've gotten really good at playing the trophy wife who doesn't know a thing about what her husband was doing." She shook her head, and the playful smile disappeared. "But I don't miss anything, Mike. For my own protection, I learned very early in my marriage to Danny that I needed to pay attention to everything."

"A very wise practice, Susan." Black nodded, more impressed by Susan than he had been prior to this conversation. He too had seen her as the stereotypical know-nothing trophy wife. The fact that she wasn't made Susan dangerous. "Have you heard from him?"

"Yes, I have. He called my sister and sent a message to me."

"What did he want?"

"He wanted the ten thousand dollars that was in the safe. I gave the money to Wesley, and he met Danny somewhere. I didn't want to know where. The less I knew about that, the better."

"You wouldn't happen to know where he might be hiding?"

"If he's still in the country, he might be hiding with a woman named Abony Shamone."

"Who is she?"

Susan blushed. "I'm embarrassed to say that Ms. Shamone is a dominatrix who Danny sees sometimes," she said, wondering what he thought her husband seeing a dominatrix said about her.

"If he's not in the country?"

"He could be anywhere in the world. But I heard him telling somebody that Elias had a place in Turks and Caicos and that he needed to get down there before that Nazzy guy got to it."

"Got to what, Susan?" Black asked, assuming that Beason was looking for the drive or the information it contained.

Susan leaned forward a little, inhaled deeply, and sighed soulfully as she stared into his eyes. "I wish I could tell you, Mike."

She had very expressive eyes. It was one of his weaknesses.

"I think I've taken up enough of your time tonight, Susan." Black stood up and so did Bobby.

"I hope I was helpful to you, Mike," she said and stood up to walk them out.

"Yes, Susan, you've been a big help. Thank you," Black said as they got to the door.

Susan opened the door and stepped out. "My pleasure. Come back anytime," she said, waving as they walked down her driveway. She went back inside and shut the door.

"She wants to fuck you," Bobby said as they walked away from the house.

"I know."

"And she doesn't try hard to keep it a secret either."

"Cassandra noticed that too," Black said as they got to the car.

"She just don't know who she's fuckin' with," Bobby laughed, and they got in. "Shy will put a bullet in her brain."

Black laughed. "Cassandra mentioned that, too."

Chapter Eleven

The Playhouse nightclub and gambling house was the next stop for Black and Bobby. Earlier in the day, he had arranged for Agent McCullough to meet him there. On top of that, Black liked to go to the Playhouse to check on Barbara. Before Black had a daughter, Barbara was the daughter he never thought he'd have, so he was just as protective of her as her father. When Barbara was informed that they were in the house, she was glad they were there because she needed some advice. Now that she had all but gotten rid of the G40s, the BBKs were moving into the area. She was going to talk to Jackie about it, but who better than her father and her uncle Mike?

There was a time when Barbara wasn't comfortable talking to her uncle about her issues. She felt that he would see her as the pampered princess she used to be who had no business in his world. It was only at the constant urgings of Jackie and Monika, who both told her how much they learned from him, that Barbara finally sought his advice.

"How did you get rid of the G40s?" Black asked.

"I invited them to a sit-down at the Playhouse, and I killed them."

"Oh," Bobby said.

Black smiled at Bobby and shook his head.

"Did I do something wrong?" Barbara asked innocently.

"No. You had a problem, and you handled it," Black said and looked at Bobby. "Same way we used to handle things back in the day."

"I know. I cut off the head, and they fell apart."

"Exactly."

"I spend a lot of time talking to my captain. She says that everything she knows she learned from you, Uncle Mike," Barbara said.

"Problem is now that you got rid of the G40s, you got a new problem," Bobby said. "A new crew is moving in to pick up the pieces."

"How do you think I should handle it?"

"Draw them in, and hit them when they least expect it," Bobby said and thought about an interesting way she could do it.

"But here's the thing, Barbara—it's gonna keep happening. Just like you dealt with the G40s and BBKs showed up," Black began.

"Somebody will show up to take the BBKs place," Barbara said.

"The next day," Bobby said.

"What you have to do is establish yourself as somebody they don't want to go at," Black suggested. "Make the next one think about the last one and think again."

"How do I do that, Uncle Mike?"

Black and Bobby looked at one another and then at Barbara. "You keep doing what you're doing, baby girl," Bobby said.

"When one tries you, you kill them," was the advice Black offered his niece.

"After a while, people will say, 'You don't want to fuck with Barbara Ray. She'll kill you sooner than she'll talk to you.'"

"And then men will fear you," Black said.

"Like you and Daddy. Nobody wanted to take you two on," Barbara said and looked at her father. He stood up.

"This is the life you've chosen for yourself. I hope you're up to it," Bobby said and held his arms out. Barbara stood up and came around her desk to hug her father. "I love you, baby girl, and know that I am always here if you need me."

"I know that, Daddy. And I love you too."

Black stood up and hugged Barbara. "I know that you're up to it."

"Thank you, Uncle Mike."

"But all you gotta do is say the word, and I will wipe these chuckleheads off the face of the earth for you."

When Barbara laughed and Black didn't, she knew that he meant it. "Thank you, Uncle Mike. I'll let you know if I need you," she said, glad to know that she had that kind of power behind her and thought about what having that kind of power would allow her to do. "But I can handle them."

Tahanee knocked on the door and stuck her head in. "Excuse me, Mr. Black, but there is a woman out here who said that you were expecting her."

"I am. Thank you, Tahanee." He looked at Barbara. "Is it all right if I use your office for a while?"

Barbara frowned. "Of course it is," she said and followed Tahanee out of the office. A few minutes later, she escorted the woman into the office.

"Thank you, Barbara."

"You're welcome, Uncle Mike." She left the office.

"Agent McCullough," Black said when she closed the door.

"What's up, Mack?" Bobby asked.

"I'm okay, Bobby."

She turned to Black. "What's going on with you?"

"How much do you know about the Albanian mob?"

"That there is one. Beyond that, I got nothing for you." She laughed. "I stick to the Italians. They're stable, predictable. Albanians, not so much. What you got?"

Black ran down for the agent what he needed her to know.

Agent McCullough laughed. "Rain ain't no joke, is she?"

"No, she's not, and Monika is Rain with weapons and tactical skills," Black said, thinking that he still hadn't heard from either of them. "See what you can find out."

Agent McCullough stood up. "Give me a day or two, and I'll get back to you."

"Thanks, Mack," he said, and the agent left the office.

"What you wanna do now?" Bobby asked.

"Let's go to La Chatte. I wanna talk to Mercedes. I remember Jada telling me once that she poached a Croatian woman from the Albanians a couple of years ago."

"You think she's still there?"

"One way to find out," he said, and after saying good-bye to Barbara, Black and Bobby left the Playhouse.

Once he saw how extremely profitable Paraíso, the casino and high-end brothel that he ran with Jada West in Nassau, was, he wanted to open the same type of high-end establishment in the city. Therefore, when Cynt was murdered, Black closed her spot and separated the women from the gambling. The women went to work at a new club called Shooters. Then Black got Jada to recruit and train the ladies and teach Mercedes how a Mike Black establishment was to be run. With the ladies in place, Black took Cynt's gambling operation, and he opened La Chatte.

"Yes, Mr. Black," Mercedes said. "She is still with us. Her name is Lucija Kovacic. Please, relax and enjoy the hospitality of the house, and as soon as she's available, I'll have her brought to my office if that's acceptable."

"Thanks, Mercedes, that will be fine."

"Send one of the ladies over with drinks," Bobby said and sat down at a table.

"It would be my pleasure, Bobby," she said and held up one finger. Two of her ladies rushed over to the table in response to the gesture.

"Yes, Mercedes?" they both said.

"See to Mr. Black's and Mr. Ray's needs."

"Yes, Mercedes," they both said.

"Enjoy yourselves, gentlemen, and I'll let you know when Lucija is available to speak with you."

"Thank you, Mercedes."

Mercedes left them at the table to enjoy Veronica Rose on vocals with the La Chatte Quintet. Elegantly dressed in a Talbot Runhof metallic cape gown and gloves, she was singing an Ella Fitzgerald–inspired version of "I Can't Give You Anything but Love."

"No, that is not Mike Black." She walked closer to the table as the quintet kept playing. "Yes, it is. Ladies and gentlemen, Mike Black and Bobby Ray are in the house tonight. Please help me welcome them," she said to a smattering of handclaps from the ladies who worked there as she sat down at the table with them.

"Hey, Mike. Hey, Bobby."

"Veronica, how are you?" Black said and kissed her gloved hand.

"Absolutely wonderful thanks to you. And that's why . . ." She stood up and sang, "'I can't give you anything but love, baby. That's the only thing I've plenty of, baby.'" She blew Black a kiss and rejoined the quintet.

It was Black who got Veronica the job at La Chatte after hearing her sing at a club where a trap had been set for him. When Black, Rain, and his brother shot their way out of there, they took Veronica with them. After years of knocking around from club to club, singing whatever others wanted her to sing, Veronica was singing the songs she wanted to sing the way she wanted to sing them, so she was eternally grateful.

It was thirty minutes later when La Chatte's hostess, Alisha Jenay, came to the table and escorted Black and Bobby to the office.

"Mr. Black, Mr. Ray, this is the woman you were asking about, Lucija Kovacic," Mercedes introduced them.

"Nice to meet you, Ms. Kovacic," Black said. "Please sit down."

"Thank you, Mr. Black."

"You used to work for the Albanian?"

"More like I was their slave, but yes. Ms. West bought my freedom from those animals."

"Where did you work out of?"

"At a small hotel bar called the Watering Hole for a man named Artie Bukuroshe."

"Thank you, Ms. Kovacic. You've been very helpful," Black said, and he and Bobby headed out.

When they got there, Black and Bobby sat outside the small hotel bar and observed the activity both inside and outside.

"How you wanna do this?" Bobby asked. "Because you know if we go in there asking for this Artie asshole, we're gonna end up shooting our way outta there."

"That's true."

"So we going in there?"

"We used to."

"We were younger and pretty stupid back then."

"That's true, too. But we'll definitely get their attention."

"Well, since we out here, might as well start some shit," Bobby said, and they got out.

"That's how you find shit out," Black said, checking his weapons as he walked.

When they got inside, it went pretty much the way they thought it would. Black and Bobby went to the bar, ordered drinks, and asked the bartender if he knew Artie Bukuroshe or where to find him. He said that he'd never heard of him, but five minutes later, he was talking to two men and pointing out Black and Bobby.

"Time to go," Black said.

Bobby paid their tab, and they walked out of the bar.

The two men waited a few seconds before following Black and Bobby out. Bobby looked over his shoulder as they crossed the street to where the car was parked. "Here they come."

"You go right. I go left," Black said, and put his hands in his pockets.

"Call it."

"Go," Black said and went to the left as Bobby went right, and both men drew their weapons and opened fire.

The two men were caught totally off guard, and Bobby shot one twice in the chest before he got his gun out. As Bobby moved behind a parked car for cover, he fired at the other man. He took cover quickly behind a car and returned Bobby's fire.

While they exchanged gunfire, Black stayed low, moving alongside the cars until he had a clear shot at the man crouched behind the car. Black fired and hit the man with one shot to the head. Then he walked up, stood over him, and put two in his chest. As Bobby walked to where his car was parked, Black looked at the bar. The window was crowded with men and women standing and watching what was taking place.

When Bobby swung around, Black got in, and they drove off.

Chapter Twelve

"I'm fine, really," Rain said on the phone to Daniella Ramsey, her physician's assistant.

"You may still be experiencing morning sickness."

"That's pretty much gone."

"You may start to feel bloated, and your breasts may start to grow."

"They have."

"And you'll want to keep eating well."

"Really, Daniella, I'm fine."

"Okay, Rain. If you have any symptoms that are out of the ordinary, you need to call me."

"I will, Daniella, but I gotta go," Rain said and ended the call.

She was at the hospital with Sapphire and her Aunt Priscilla, so when she hung up the phone, they both were staring at her, and Priscilla had questions.

"Who was that, Lorraine?" her aunt asked.

"That was my doctor's assistant."

"It sounded like she was concerned about you. Is everything all right?"

"It's nothing. I hurt my back while I was looking for Sapphire," Rain said instead of telling her aunt that she was pregnant.

"She had to fight some guy off, Mommy," Sapphire added.

"But I'm fine."

She looked at Sapphire, who thought that, despite the problems she was having with Carter, Rain should have the baby. She could tell by the look in her eyes that she was dying to tell her mother that Rain was pregnant, so it was time to get out of there.

"I'm about to get outta here," she said and stood up.

"You going to have that overdue talk?" Sapphire asked. She also told Rain that whether she was going to have the baby or not, she needed to talk to Carter.

"No. I'm going to the office. Going to see if the Albanians reached out about getting that drive back." She went to the bed and kissed Priscilla on the cheek. "You rest. I'll be back as soon as I can."

"You do what you gotta do to end this. We'll be fine here, Lorraine."

Rain looked at Sapphire and leaned close to her. "I'm gonna talk to him. Let me get past this first, okay?"

"Okay." Sapphire hugged her and whispered, "You two take care of yourselves."

"Funny," Rain said on her way out of the room with Alwan.

On the way down in the elevator, Rain took out her phone and started to call Carter. She was going to tell him to meet her at the office so they could talk. Then she shook her head and put her phone back in her pocket.

"Change your mind?"

"Don't fuck with me, Alwan. I am not in the mood," Rain said as the doors opened, and they got off the elevator.

As Alwan drove Rain to the office, she was surprised that the Albanians hadn't made another attempt to get the drive, especially now that she knew what information it contained. It didn't make sense. The Albanians pushed, and The Family pushed back. The only thing that Rain could think of was that the Albanians had paused to see just who was pushing back against them.

When she got to the office, Carla hit her with the one thing she didn't want to hear. "Black wants to talk to you."

"I know." When she got back to the hospital, it was the first thing that had come flying out of her aunt's mouth.

"Bobby Ray and Mike Black came by to see me while you were gone," she had said. "Mike wants you and Monika to call him."

"I'll call him in a minute. How are you?" Rain had asked and purposely had never gotten around to calling him back.

Monika came into the operation center from her office. When she got back from blowing up the Tirana Gentlemen's Club, Carla gave her Black's message. She made the same choice that Rain did. "I'll call him back in a minute. Have you found out anything else about the Troka Clan?"

Therefore, when they saw each other, each had the same question for the other.

"You talk to Black yet?" Rain asked.

"No. Did you?"

"No."

"I knew he really just wanted to talk to you."

"You're right." Rain sat down. "But I do need to talk to him," she said and was about to reach for the office phone so she could talk to him on a secure line.

"Before you do that, sunshine, let's stop and think for a second."

"Okay. What are we thinking about?"

"You know as soon as you talk to him, he's gonna shut us down."

"Yup, he sure is."

"You done?" Monika asked.

"You done?" Rain asked.

"I'm asking you, sunshine."

"Don't fuck with me, Monika. I know you got some-place for us. So what you got?"

Monika grinned. "I got their whole ensemble to choose from. It's just a matter of how bad you wanna hurt them."

"What you mean?"

"In two hours, there's a shipment of heroin coming in en route to Canada."

Rain shook her head, although blowing up a shipment of heroin was appealing. "That would cost them too much money. That's the shit you go to war over, and I ain't trying to go to war." Rain smiled. "I just wanna fuck with them."

"Got you. So I got this warehouse. According to their data, there was a shipment of weapons going to an outfit in Jacksonville, Florida, that they should have cleared out of this warehouse last night."

"What's there now?"

"As far as I can tell from their data, nothing," Carla advised.

"Minimum cost, low security. I think this spot is ideal for what you wanna do," Monika said.

"All right, let's do it."

When they got there, Rain grabbed a couple of HK433s and some extra clips, and Monika got enough C-4 and detonators to get the job done. Rain shut the trunk, and the pair headed into the shadows toward the warehouse. Once they reached the structure, Rain covered while Monika set the C-4 and detonators.

"Somebody's coming," Rain said as one man stepped to the dock armed with an AK.

Monika kept quietly doing what she was doing, and Rain took aim until he walked away. "I thought Carla said that there was no security."

"She said low security. He should be the only one, and we'll take care of him once we have everything set. We only have two more to go."

Once that explosive was set, they moved on to the next spot. When they got to the stairs that led inside the warehouse, Monika got to work. She had just finished when a man appeared at the top of the stairs and opened fire on them with a semiautomatic weapon. Rain and Monika immediately sought better cover as the gunman sprayed the area.

When Rain made it to cover, she raised her weapon and shot him in the head. When he went down, another man appeared at the top of the steps and began firing, forcing them to seek cover again.

"Cover me!"

While Rain exchanged fire with the shooter, Monika moved out. Staying low, she moved to get a better angle on the shooter. When she was in position, Monika rose up and fired, taking him out with a shot in the chest.

"We need to get outta here," Rain said.

"Right."

They moved out, but they had to immediately retreat and run for cover, as two more men with automatic weapons began firing at them. Monika and Rain were pinned down and taking heavy fire. Monika raised her weapon and opened fire, hitting one of the gunmen. Rain got to her feet and took down the other shooter.

"This is a lot more security than we were expecting," Rain said once she came out from her cover.

"Maybe they upped their security since we're fuckin' with them," Monika said as she saw two more men coming at them, firing.

Rain and Monika returned fire on them as they ran toward the gate, but the gunfire from two shooters sent them rushing for cover as they sprayed the area with bullets. As the shooting continued, Rain and Monika separated so they could isolate one of the shooters and get him in a crossfire. Their adversaries separated to pursue them but quickly lost Monika. Rain fired a couple of shots, then ran for better cover behind a truck.

While Rain exchanged shots with them, Monika crawled along the ground. With their attention focused on Rain, Monika was able to keep moving until she had gotten behind one of them. When he turned toward Monika, she opened fire. He went down from the cluster of shots that hit him in the chest.

Now that only one shooter remained, Rain stepped out and took him down with one shot to the head. Rain walked over to the one she killed, stood over him, and put two in his chest.

"Let's get the fuck outta here and blow this place before any more of these muthafuckas show up," Monika said as she walked away with Rain.

Once they had driven to what Monika considered a safe distance, she parked the car. Rain and Monika got out and looked at the warehouse.

"Hit it."

Monika pressed the detonate button on her tablet, and they watched the warehouse explode. And then Rain and Monika stood there and watched it burn.

"I got a little pyromaniac in me," Rain said.

"Me too, sunshine. I like to watch shit burn too, so I ain't mad at you at all," Monika said, and they watched the warehouse burn until they heard the sirens in the distance. "You gonna call Black now?"

"Yeah," Rain said and took out her phone.

Chapter Thirteen

As Bobby drove away from the Watering Hole, he looked in his rearview mirror. "We got a tail, Mike."

Black looked back. "Looks like they're keeping their distance. They just wanna follow us, find out who we are." He smiled and shook his head. "I don't think so, Bob. They wanna follow us, so let's lead them somewhere."

"Anyplace in particular?"

Black thought about it. "Let's go see Chance," he said and took out his phone as Bobby drove toward Clay's Garage, the chop shop and auto junkyard that was run by Chance.

"Clay's," Chance answered.

"What's up, Chance? This is Mike."

"Sup, Mike, how's it going?"

"It's lovely. Listen, me and Bobby are coming, and we're coming with company. They're in a Toyota Highlander. Be a good man and open the gate for us."

"I'll make sure they feel welcome."

"Thank you, sir. See you in a while," Black said and ended the call.

"You're in a good mood," Bobby said.

"No, Bob, I'm not. Rain and Monika tried to return the fuckin' drive, and these muthafuckas shot Priscilla. Dishonorable people don't get to be treated honorably."

"You don't have to explain to me. I was just saying that you're in a good mood, that's all. But you say you're not. Even though you're sitting over there, smiling like a little kid, you're not in a good mood."

"I'm mad, Bob, but I'm having a good time. We don't do this type of shit anymore."

"You're the one deep into playing legitimate business-man."

Black turned slowly and looked at Bobby.

"That's right, I said it. You and Shy are both playing at being legitimate. But let some shit happen, and all of a sudden Clair Huxtable turns into Pam Grier, and out comes the PLR22."

"And she'll be looking for a big purse that matches her outfit to put it in."

"And you. This is who you are, Mike, not some fuckin' businessman. You are vicious muthafuckin' Black," Bobby said, pounding the steering wheel to emphasize each word. "You kill people. That's what you do."

"I am not even going to attempt to argue with you."

"Because you know I'm right. Every time I come to the office, you are sitting there bored out of your goddamn mind."

"Not all the time."

Bobby shook his head. "Do you know how weak that shit sounded? 'Not all the time.' Yes, Mike, all the mutha-fuckin' time. Admit it." Bobby pointed at him. "You're a killer. That's who you are, not a businessman."

"Why don't you tell me how you really feel, Bob?"

"I just did."

"And you're right."

"I know I am."

"Most days I'm just there, or I'm hanging out in Cassandra's office, talking."

"Y'all might as well go home and talk."

"Most days we do."

"You're proving my point, Mike. That shit y'all are trying to do is nice, and I'm sure M and Joanne are happy as peaches that y'all are"—Bobby took his hands off the wheel long enough to make air quotes—"quote unquote 'retired,' but the only one y'all are fooling is Mansa."

Black laughed as they approached a darkened Clay's Garage.

"Everybody else knows who the two of you really are."

"Who are we really, Bob?"

"Mr. and Mrs. I'll Kill a Muthafucka," Bobby said as the gate at Clay's Garage opened, and he drove into the darkened yard. As they hoped, the Highlander followed them in, and the gate closed behind them.

Inside the Highlander, the two men looked out their windows and saw the heavily armed men standing on either side. They knew they had made a mistake following them in. And now they were about to die for that mistake. There was a car carrier blocking their path, so they had to stop.

Black and Bobby, along with Chance, came around the car carrier as their men moved in on the vehicle. Once their men had taken the men from the Highlander and disarmed them, they walked them in front of Black and Bobby, and they were made to kneel before them.

"There are two ways this can go," Black began. "I could send one of you back to deliver a message, or I could just shoot you both now and go have a drink." Black took out his gun and shot them both. "Let's go get a drink."

"That's right! That's vicious muthafuckin' Black!" Bobby shouted as they walked back to his car. "Now ain't you having fun? I know I am."

"More fun than we've had in years," he said, knowing that the thing to do was to let one go to deliver a message.

"Damn right. Where you wanna go drink at?"

"I don't know. Where haven't you been in a while?"

"I haven't been anywhere in a while, Mike. I haven't even been to Impressions in a while."

"You wanna go there?"

"No. Crowd's too young, and that's why I haven't been there in a while. What about you?"

"I go to Conversations all the time."

"So I hear."

"What you mean?"

"That I hear you and Jackie spend a lot of time alone together in her office."

"What are you trying to say?"

"I ain't trying to say shit. That's just the word around The Family." Black looked confused and a little annoyed, so Bobby explained. "Jackie is the teacher's pet, and the teacher spends a lot of time with his pet."

Black laughed. "Seriously?"

"You know muthafuckas ain't got shit else to do but talk. You ain't been retired long enough to forget that."

"True. Niggas ain't got shit else to do, especially in peacetime."

"Especially since niggas got tired of making shit up about you, Jada, and Shy." Bobby laughed because the stories ranged from threesomes to murder plots. "Which reminds me, I haven't seen the lovely Ms. West in a while. How is she?"

"You haven't seen Jada up here because she got shot," Black laughed. "She says we play too rough up here."

"Then Nassau's the best place for her."

"For so many reasons."

"What you mean?"

"I mean, Cassandra is happier when Jada is in another country."

"I thought they got along now."

"Both of them are great at playing nice, but I know for a fact that Cassandra would rather shoot Jada in the head than talk to her."

"Then why didn't she just leave her to die instead of insisting that you couldn't leave her?"

"I have asked her that question more than once."

"What does she say?"

"She says she doesn't know why and gets mad at me."

Bobby shook his head. "So where we going?"

"The West Coast games are still on. Roll by Romans. Let's see what's up there."

It was twenty minutes later when Bobby parked down the street from Romans. They got out and were walking to the pizzeria when Black's phone rang. "Hello, Rain."

"Where you at?"

"I'm at Romans."

Fuck! "I'm on my way," Rain said.

"Bring Monika with you."

"Yes, sir." Rain glanced at Monika and ended the call. "He wants me to bring you with me."

"Good. Let's go," Monika said. "All I'll get outta Black is a stern look."

"But I'm the boss of The Family." Rain felt the weight of the power and responsibility that she carried. "I'm supposed to keep the peace so everybody can keep making money."

"It's what we get up every day for." Monika paused and shrugged her shoulders. "At least, that's what they tell me." She giggled because she wasn't in the moneymaking end of The Family.

Rain shook her head because Monika could be foolish when she wanted to be. "Let's go."

After one last look at the warehouse, she and Monika got in the car and went to meet Black at Romans. Now Rain had two reasons not to be looking forward to this.

Why did he have to want to meet at Romans? she asked herself as Monika drove off.

Romans exploded when Black and Bobby walked in the door. Everybody in the joint wanted to shake hands or bump fists or just be around the true bosses of The Family. Everybody wanted to buy Black and Bobby a drink—drinks they didn't turn down—and everybody wanted to talk. Some members of The Family there had never actually seen Black or Bobby. They stood in awe of the legends they'd only heard about.

Of course, there were those who wanted something that they could only get from Black, or at least that was the way they made it seem. Naturally, there were those who needed a favor. They were buying drinks too, while some others just spoke so others would know that they were in the room the night Mike Black and Bobby Ray came to Romans.

Carter had been sitting alone, thinking about the situation with Kojo's men, when he heard the commotion. He flipped on the monitor, and he saw Black and Bobby. Surrounded. He got up and went out there to greet them, but the crowd was thick, so he decided that it would be easier to wait for them to make their way to him. Therefore, he had no idea that Rain had come to Romans.

"There must be something big about to happen tonight!" Black heard somebody shout when Rain and Monika came in and began pushing their way through the crowd.

"There they are," Bobby said when the pair made it to the table.

"What's up, Black? What's up, Bobby?" Monika said and sat down at the table.

"What's going down, Monika?" Bobby said.

"What we drinking?" she asked and looked around. "Somebody bring me a drink." She was having way too much fun with this.

Black hadn't said a word. He just sat there looking at Rain, and she stood there looking at him. He got up and stood in front of her. "Let's talk in the office."

"Yes, sir," Rain said and looked at the crowd surrounding them. She took out her gun and fired one shot at the ceiling. It got everybody's attention, including Carter's. "Make a hole!" Rain shouted, and the crowd at Romans erupted in cheers and laughter.

"Rain Robinson is in the house!" one or two of them yelled and began barking, but they made a hole as she requested.

Black looked at Monika. She was still sitting down at the table. "You too, Monika."

She stood up. "But nobody brought me a drink yet," she said, and a man rushed up and handed her one. "Thank you. Lead the way."

As Rain led the way to the office, Carter saw her coming and took a deep breath. He was glad she was there because they needed to talk about what was going on with Kojo, but he knew, knowing Rain the way that he did, that she would find a way to slip out of there without talking to him. Especially with Black and Bobby there.

"What's up, Mike? What's up, Bobby?" Carter asked and shook their hands. He nodded at Rain, and she rolled her eyes. "What brings you two to Romans?"

Black looked at Rain. "Seems that I came here to talk to her."

"We need to use your office," Rain said and walked by Carter.

"Be my guest," he said and followed everybody into his office.

"You wanna tell me about it?" Black began when Carter closed the door.

Rain told Black and Bobby what happened to set the events in motion, from that first call from Millie and having to fight off somebody at Sapphire's apartment, to the fire they set at Overseas Air, to blowing up the Tirana Gentlemen's Club, to the shootout they'd just left. "They shot my aunt, Black. We were there to return the drive and get my aunt back, and they shot her. I know that I should have done something to deescalate the situation, but I was mad, so I made sure they knew that my family ain't to be fucked with."

"Carla says that you're on these guys too," Monika said.

"They might be responsible for the death of a friend of mine. The drive that they are so desperate to get back was taken from them by Elias Colton, and that's what got him killed."

"Who the fuck is Elias Colton?" Rain asked.

"The dead muthafucka who set all this in motion," he said and told them what he'd been able to piece together. Then he told them what he and Bobby had been doing.

"No wonder you ain't mad at her," Monika said. "You two been acting up."

"Acting like we grown or some shit," Bobby added, laughing.

"So from now on, nobody does shit. We got what they want. Sooner or later . . . probably sooner after tonight," Black said, and everybody laughed. "But they'll come to us. Is that understood?"

"Understood," Rain said.

Black stood up. "Come on. Carter's buying," he said and led everyone out of the office.

As everybody went to the bar to get a drink, Rain told Black that she wanted to drop by the hospital to check on her aunt and cousin.

"After all we did tonight, I just want to make sure they're all right," she said, and Carter watched her and Monika leave Romans without her saying a word to him, just as he expected.

So Carter told Black and Bobby what he'd found out about Kojo, and then he spent the rest of the night getting drunk and telling old stories. But Carter was thinking about Rain, her pregnancy, and the fact that she wouldn't talk to him.

Chapter Fourteen

The scene was quiet at Montefiore Hospital. Monika's five armed operatives were still on site for Sapphire and Aunt Priscilla's protection. Team one was made up of Beta and Gamma, and they were covering the entrances as well as the lobby area. Team two was Delta and Epsilon, and they were stationed in the hallway outside the room. Alpha was their team leader, and she was the floater and had positioned herself in the waiting room on Aunt Priscilla's floor. It was a good and capable team, but they were security contractors with military experience, licensed to carry firearms, who worked for the security company and not members of The Family. However, when four men who met the profile Monika had given them passed through the lobby, team one responded.

"Beta to Alpha."

"Go ahead with your traffic."

"Four Caucasian men just entered the hospital, and they are heading toward the main bank of elevators."

"Acknowledged. Gamma, maintain your position. Beta, rendezvous with me on five."

"Acknowledged. En route."

"Standby, team two," Alpha said and took out her phone to call Monika.

"This is Omega."

"Omega, this is Alpha. Four Caucasian men just entered the hospital and are heading toward the main bank of elevators. Assuming defensive positioning."

"Acknowledged, Alpha. Sunshine and I are en route. If at all possible, do not engage."

"Acknowledged, Omega."

"What's up?" Rain asked, and Monika drove faster.

"Four men just came into the hospital."

When the elevator doors opened on the fifth floor, Alpha was standing there when the four men got off and turned toward Aunt Priscilla's room.

"Alpha to Delta," she said, moving in behind them as they walked.

"Go ahead."

"I have four Caucasian males advancing on your position."

"Acknowledged."

When Beta reached the fifth floor, he immediately headed toward Aunt Priscilla's room. Therefore, when the four males reached the room, Delta and Epsilon were waiting for them. The men stopped and the stare down began. One of the men glanced over his shoulder. By that time, Alpha and Beta were behind them. As her team maintained their positions, Alpha approached the men.

"Can I help you gentlemen with something?" she asked as she tapped the handle of her holstered gun.

Being stuck in the middle and wishing to avoid a confrontation, one said, "No problem. Wrong floor." They backed down and left the area. Alpha and Beta followed them to the elevator and watched them get on.

"Alpha to Gamma."

"Gamma."

"You've got four Caucasian males coming your way. Beta and I are right behind them in the next elevator," she advised.

Therefore, when the four males reached the ground floor and the elevator doors opened, Gamma was there waiting for them. A few seconds later, the other elevator door opened, and Gamma was joined by Alpha and Beta. The four men were followed out of the hospital without incident.

"Omega," Monika answered when Alpha called.

"Situation resolved without incident. Subjects in question have left the hospital."

"Acknowledged, Alpha. We are five minutes out. I'll expect your full report."

"Acknowledged."

"Good job, team leader," Monika said to her and ended the call.

"Wasn't that sweet of you?" Rain said.

"It was her first time in command. I think that positive reinforcement is important."

"I hear you."

Monika had almost reached the hospital when an Audi Q7 cut them off and crashed into the driver's side fender, forcing them into the cars parked on the street. Two men got out and opened fire. It was then that a Land Rover came to a screeching halt behind them, and two more men got out, firing at Monika and Rain. As shells bounced off the bullet-resistant vehicle, Monika and Rain shook it off.

"You all right?" Monika asked Rain as she got out her guns.

When the Audi hit them, Rain hit her head pretty hard against the window. "I'm all right," she said and released the catch to gain access to her trunk.

Because she hated being outgunned at any time, Rain had an arsenal in her trunk. She had two AR-15s, two of her favorite HK433s, two M4 carbines, an M203 grenade launcher, a Barrett M82 sniper rifle, concussion and fragmentation grenades, and enough C-4, timers, detonators, and everything else she'd need to blow up whatever she wanted.

Monika jumped out and opened fire with her two nines and caused their attackers to back off and retreat to cover. Rain got the two HK433s, some magazines, and a couple of concussion grenades before she got out of the car.

Monika rose up and tried to get off a shot with her nine, but she was outgunned. She dropped back behind the car and looked over at Rain. She pulled the pin and threw a concussion grenade at the Land Rover and the other at the Audi. The explosives disoriented their attackers. Rain tossed Monika an AR-15 and opened fire. She shot one in the chest before she returned to cover.

As bullets bounced off of the car and the wall behind them, Rain and Monika shot it out with the three remaining ambushers.

"Shit!" Monika shouted, and then she raised the AR and fired three times. Each shot hit one of their attackers, and he fell to the ground.

Rain stood up, tossed another grenade at the men, and then fired on them until the HK433 was empty and one of the men went down. Monika took a deep breath before she came up shooting at the last man. As he tried to run, she fired but only hit him in the shoulder. He was about to return fire when Rain shot him in the head.

With all of their attackers down, Rain and Monika walked up on each one and put bullets in their heads.

"Black was right. They're gonna come to us."

"They're gonna keep coming until they get that drive," Monika said.

"I know. And the muthafuckas can have it." Rain laughed. "All they gotta do is not shoot first, and they can have that shit."

Chapter Fifteen

It was five in the morning when one of Carter's men dropped Black off at his house. Both he and Bobby had drunk way too much. Because they had so much fun that night, Carter made somebody drive them home. While they were there, Carter took the opportunity to talk to Black and Bobby about what was going on with Ryder and Truck. Since he knew that Jackie had Marvin and Baby Chris looking into how Kojo's operation was set up, he had gone to Conversations earlier that evening to talk with her about it.

"Black was right," Jackie began.

"He usually is," Carter added.

"Kojo's program is structured like a mafia family from boss, underboss, consigliere, capos, and soldiers. His consigliere's a white woman named Giordena Petrocelli, and she came courtesy of Angelo. Near as Marvin and Baby Chris can tell, she reports directly to Joey Toscano."

"That's Angelo's main guy, right?"

"The same. She is always with him, and she is always in his ear. His head of security, Brendon Walker, functions as underboss. He's never far from Kojo either, but he basically manages the different parts of their operation."

"Other than the dope game, what are they into?"

"Gambling, prostitution, extortion, protection."

"Just like a mafia family," Carter said.

"Just like us without the drugs," Jackie pointed out, and she continued. "Jerome Dorsey runs the gambling.

Jackson Hill's a gorilla pimp he met while he was in prison. Runs prostitution for him. Kevin Franklin runs extortion, protection rackets, that type of shit. He's one of Joey's guys."

"Who runs his drug operation?"

"He's pretty hands-on as far as the dope game is concerned. He's got four lieutenants. Arron Copeland and Shanice Hardaway deal with his more upscale markets, but he relies on two brothers, Andrew and Rodney Mack, to deal with the drug gangs."

Carter smiled. "Any relation to Keisha and Connie Mack?" he asked because the mother of Bobby's daughter Tenikka was Keisha Mack.

"No. But wouldn't that be some shit?"

"It would." Carter paused and sipped his drink. "Which one does Ryder have beef with?"

"That would be Rodney Mack. Calls himself Truck," Jackie said, and then she let Carter know that Monika had surveillance teams in place and ready to go. Carla was already up on all of the major players' phones. They were just waiting on the word go to get started. After he thanked her for the information, Carter left and went back to Romans. He had planned to tell Rain, but he wasn't expecting Black and Bobby that night, so to Carter, this worked out better.

Since Jackie had already told him everything that Carter just told them a week ago, Black said, "Stay on top of it."

Bobby raised his glass. "To staying on top of it."

And they drank to staying on top of it as they had everything else that night at Romans.

Therefore, when Black got out of the car, he had to stand still, focus, and steady himself before he started walking toward the house. As quietly as he could, Black unlocked the door, went inside, and made it upstairs to his bedroom.

He opened the door and went into the room, proud of the fact that he had made it that far without falling or making any noise because he was fucked up. Black looked at Shy sleeping peacefully on her side. He stood there for a second or two listening to the sound of her breathing and admiring the shape of her hip.

My wife is so muthafuckin' fine.

Then he went into the bathroom to get undressed so he wouldn't wake her up. When he came out of the bathroom, he sat down on the bed as gently as he could.

"Did you have a good time?" Shy asked as he lay next to her.

"I did."

"Good. You needed that," she said, rolled to his chest, and went back to sleep.

He put his arm around her, kissed her forehead, thought about going up in her, and then he passed the fuck out.

When her alarm went off a couple of hours later, knowing her husband would be no help with the morning ritual, Shy got up and got to it. Fortunately for her, Mansa was still asleep, so she took him and laid him on the bed with her mother before moving on to wake up Michelle and Easy. While M prepared breakfast and lunch for the children, Shy showered and dressed in a two-tone Alexander McQueen Prince of Wales suit and Alexander McQueen leather ankle-strap sandals. Once she was dressed, Chuck took her to the offices of Prestige Capital and Associates.

"Good morning, Mrs. Black," Lenecia said when Shy came through the door. "How are you today?"

"I'm fine, Lenecia. How are you?"

"Doing great today," she said, waving as Shy went to her office.

"Good morning, everybody," Shy said when she came in and headed for her office. On the way, she stuck her head in the door of Reeva Duckworth, the shipping manager at CAMB Overseas Importers. "Hey, Reeva. Stop by my office when you get a minute. I wanna talk about any technical requirements we might run into when we start exporting into the new markets."

"Give me around fifteen minutes to wrap this up, and I'll be right in," she said, and Shy went on to her office.

There really wouldn't be a CAMB Overseas Importers without Reeva. It was her job to ensure that CAMB Overseas Importers shipments arrived at their destinations on time. She coordinated incoming and outgoing shipments and negotiated transportation costs with carriers to stay within budget. Reeva was the first person Shy hired, and she was her most valuable employee. Shy was so impressed with Reeva that she hired her over lunch at their first interview. During the years that they'd worked together, Reeva and Shy had gotten very close.

"I like that dress on you," Shy said of the burnt orange Marigold Phillip Lim flared shirtdress that Reeva was wearing when she came into Shy's office and sat down in one of the plush chairs in front of the desk.

"Thank you. It was on sale, so you know I had to have it."

"So talk to me. What challenges related to technical regulations are we gonna run into?"

"Naturally, we'll need to meet and provide conformity assessment results and certifications, and we'll need to factor in taxes and fees that may apply."

"That means calculating the right price and being cost competitive is going to be more important for these markets."

"Yes." Reeva nodded. "No customs duties or taxes will be assessed at the time or at the point of importation for express shipments valued at or below a fixed amount set out under the law."

"Each destination country will have their own tariff schedule to classify the goods, right?" Shy asked.

"They will," Reeva said, smiling because Shy's knowledge of her business was increasing. She knew nothing about the shipping business when she hired Reeva, so she had come a long way. "That's why I think it might be a good idea to hire a customs broker to help move our goods across borders with more certainty," she suggested.

"I was thinking the same thing. Let's make that happen as soon as we can," Shy said, satisfied that Reeva had covered all the bases as she always did.

After they talked over the management of the process, and whose responsibility it would be, Reeva went back to her office to prepare for their meeting later that day.

"Good morning, and welcome to Prestige Capital and Associates," Lenecia said, smiling brightly as she always did. "How may I help you today?"

The detectives took out their badges. "Detectives Mitchell and Harmon to see Erykah Morgan," Diane said.

"Welcome back, Detective Mitchell. If you wouldn't mind having a seat, I will let Erykah know that you're here."

"Thank you," Diane said, and the detectives went to sit down.

Since the detectives agreed that it was time that they started taking the advice of a killer, they came to ask Black why he thought it was deeper than Albert and Gayle Eager from the beginning. Earlier that morning, they questioned Lule Vata about the warehouse where Andrea Frazier's body was found. He came with a lawyer, who claimed that Vata was not able to speak English. Through his attorney, Vata said that the warehouse had been vacant for years and he knew nothing about the body. Since there was nothing to tie him to Andrea Frazier, Daniel Beason, or Elias Colton, he was released. While his lawyer was there, he paid the bail for Ismail Flamur and arranged for him to be released while he was awaiting trial on the burglary charge.

"Erykah Morgan?" Jack asked when they sat down.

"She is his executive assistant."

"Excuse me," Jack said, sat back, and picked up a magazine.

Once the detectives were seated, Lenecia called Erykah to let her know that the detectives were there. Since Black hadn't told her that he was expecting a visit from the police, Erykah started to have Lenecia tell the detective that he wasn't there. Especially since he wasn't. But since it was Detective Mitchell, and she'd heard him say that his door was always open for her, Erykah decided it may be best to call before she had Lenecia dismiss them.

Black was still asleep when the phone began ringing. At first, the ringing seemed out of place in the dream he was having, and then he realized his phone was actually ringing. He thought about ignoring it, but since very few people had the number and even fewer actually used it, he answered it.

"Hello."

"I am so sorry to wake you up, Mike," Erykah said apologetically.

"It's okay, Erykah. I needed to get up anyway." He had told Bobby that he wanted to go see Quentin's ex-wife, Leslie, that morning. "What's up?" Black looked at the time and knew that Bobby was probably still knocked out.

"Detective Mitchell and her partner are in the lobby."

"Interesting."

"I know that you said that your door was always open for Detective Mitchell, so I wasn't sure what I should do."

"It's okay, Erykah. You did the right thing. Here's what I want you to do."

It was about fifteen minutes after that when Erykah got up from her desk and started for the lobby.

"That's her." Jack and Diane stood up when she came into the area. "Good morning, Ms. Morgan," Diane said as Erykah approached.

"Good morning, Detective Mitchell," Erykah said and shook hands with Diane.

"This is my partner, Detective Harmon."

"Nice to meet you, Ms. Morgan." Jack shook hands with her as well.

"I am sorry to have kept you waiting for so long," Erykah said. "How can I help you today?"

"Is Mr. Black in? I'd like to ask him some questions," Diane said.

"I'm sorry, Detective Mitchell, but Mr. Black isn't in the office this morning."

"Do you expect him in today?" Jack said.

"No, Mr. Black will not be in the office today." Erykah smiled. "However, I have spoken with Mr. Black, and he gave me a message to give you, Detective Mitchell."

"What's the message?" Diane asked.

"Next time make an appointment," Erykah said, and she paused, smiling, before she said, "Is there anything I can do for you?"

Diane smiled. "I'd like to make an appointment."

"Do you have a card?" Erykah asked, and Diane handed her one. "Thank you, Detective Mitchell. Once I've spoken with Mr. Black, I will call you with a date and time."

"Thank you, Ms. Morgan," Diane said, and Erykah watched as the detectives left Prestige Capital and Associates.

Chapter Sixteen

It was after one in the afternoon when Black woke up again, and it was at least thirty minutes after that before he moved. When he went downstairs, M and Joanne were sitting in the living room, and Mansa was having a ball running back and forth between them.

"Afternoon, ladies," he said and picked up Mansa. "And you, my man." Black raised Mansa over his head. "How's my big boy today?"

"You want something to eat, Michael?" M asked.

"Whatever you have ready. I don't want you to go to any trouble."

M got up as Black continued flying Mansa around the room and went in the kitchen to cook her son something to eat. Since she had cooked a brisket of beef the night before for the family's dinner, she sliced off some and served it to him on a Kaiser roll.

He had promised to drop by to see Leslie Hunter, Quentin's ex-wife, but she said that something came up at the last minute. "That's okay, Leslie. I really just wanted to tell you again how sorry I am for your loss."

"Thank you, Mike."

"And if there is anything that I can ever do for you, please, Leslie, all you have to do is ask."

"Thank you, Mike. How are you doing? I know this hasn't been easy for you."

"No, it hasn't, but I'm keeping myself busy."

"Sometimes that helps," Leslie said. "But again, thank you for checking on me, Mike, but I really have to run."

Then Black called Bobby. When he didn't answer, probably still passed out after last night, Black rounded up William and went to see Elaine Cargill, the current president of the Association of Black Businesses. She was Martin Marshall's choice to lead the association.

"What were Elias and Daniel involved in?" Black asked her.

"Honestly, Mike, I have no idea. But if you wanna know what I think . . ." Elaine said, and then she spent the next half hour telling Black how much she didn't know before he left her office.

His next stop was the office of Joseph Connor, the former president of the Association of Black Businesses. Connor ran a cyber security company. He and Elias Colton never got along during his years as president. That may or may not have had something to do with the fact that Colton had been fucking Connor's wife, Georgia, behind his back for years.

"What can I do for you, Mike?"

"You can tell me what Elias and Daniel were involved in."

"Honestly, Mike, I think that they were involved with some Albanians in some type of smuggling business. What they were smuggling, I have no idea."

"What makes you think they were in the smuggling business?"

"A few years ago, this was before you joined the association, the two of them came to me about a shipping business opportunity they wanted me to invest in because of my expertise in security. You know how Elias was. He tried to slick talk me, and then he said that security was crucial to the success of the operation. Then Daniel told me how much return on my investment I would make within the first year. Then they introduced me to the guy they were partnering with—"

"The Albanian," Black said.

"Yeah, and he just rubbed me the wrong way. The whole damn thing seemed too shady, so I walked away," Connor said.

"You remember what the Albanian guy's name was?"

"Lendina Neziri. Some people you just don't forget."

"Thank you, Joseph. You've been a big help."

Joseph sat back and smiled. "Much more help than Elaine could ever be to you."

Black sat back. "Say what you wanna say, Joseph."

"I know that you backed Elaine for the presidency over me because of the run-ins I've had with Martin. I understand that. But please let Martin know that I'm a team guy and I can be of use to him too."

"I'm sure Martin will be glad to hear that." Black stood up. "I know I'm glad to hear it."

Joseph stood up and shook Black's hand. "That's good to hear, Mike," he said. Joseph escorted Black out of his office, confident that he was in a better position than he was when Mike Black had walked into his office.

When Black left Connor's office, he wanted to go by Wanda's safe house so he could talk to Rain in private. There were too many people around the night before, and on top of that, they were dealing with the Albanians, so he let it go. But he was riding with William, and if he went to talk to Rain, they'd be late picking up the children. Michelle and Easy were surprised and excited when their father and William picked them up at the Onyx Academy of Higher Learning.

Later that evening, when Shy got home from work, M served dinner. Because it was one of her son's favorites, M made meatloaf with mac and cheese, green beans, coleslaw, and fresh cucumber and chili salad.

"Bobby's not coming for dinner tonight?" M asked as the family gathered.

"I haven't heard from him today," Black said and pulled out the chair for Shy.

"Probably had as much fun as you did last night," Shy said and sat down at the table.

"He did," he said and went to sit down. "He put something on my mind last night."

"What was that?"

"I'll tell you about it after dinner," Black said and sat down.

"Why can't you talk about it over dinner?" Michelle asked her father, and then she looked at her mother.

"Yeah, Daddy," Easy said. "You said the dinner table is a place for discussion."

"Maybe because it's not for teenagers to hear," Joanne said.

"No, Joanne, they're right. This is a family discussion." He looked at Mansa and smiled. *The only one that y'all are fooling is Mansa.* "Say grace, Easy."

"Bless us, O God. Bless our food and our drink. Since you redeemed us so dearly and delivered us from evil, as you gave us a share in this food so may you give us a share in eternal life. Amen."

"Amen," everyone said.

Michelle picked up the coleslaw. "So what did Uncle Bobby say?"

"Let me start by saying that, well, you know that your mother and I haven't always been . . . I mean, we were—"

"Daddy," Michelle said to stop him, "we know what you and Mommy used to do."

Easy nodded, and M wondered where he was going with this.

"Thank you, Michelle. But we've tried to put that life behind us so the three of you would have a better life and for all of you to be safe. That is the most important thing in the world to me." He pointed. "This family."

"What did he say, Michael?" Shy asked.

"He said that you and I are both just playing at being legitimate business people but that's not who we are. He said that if something happens"—Black pointed at Shy—"Clair Huxtable turns into Pam Grier."

Joanne laughed. "That's true, Sandy," she said as she fed Mansa.

"Who is Clair Huxtable?" Easy asked.

"Who is Pam Grier?" Michelle asked.

"Before your time," M said, but she agreed too. It wasn't too long ago that it wouldn't take much for Shy to grab her Beretta and hit the street.

"I don't know about that, Michael," Shy may have said, but she knew it was true too. When somebody blew up their house, everyone involved felt Shy's wrath.

"IIe said that the only one we're fooling is Mansa because everybody else knows who we are."

"Who are we?" Shy asked.

"Excuse my language at the dinner table, but you and I are Mr. and Mrs. I'll Kill a Muthafucka."

Shy smiled, and then she repeated, "I don't know about that, Michael." But once again, she knew it was the truth. "People can change."

"And we have changed, Cassandra." He thought back to the years he'd spent tracking down and killing all the people he'd thought were involved in what he was led to believe was Shy's murder. "But if something were to happen to any one of you, I would turn into Vicious Black."

M dropped her head into her hands.

"Vicious Black?" Easy asked.

"It's what they used to call Daddy," Michelle told her brother.

"That makes me Vicious Black Jr.," Easy said proudly, and M's head returned to the palms of her hands.

"No, Easy. It doesn't," Black said quickly and firmly. "That is the point of all that your mother and I are trying to do now. So that neither of you will grow up to be me."

"Or me," Shy said, looking at Michelle.

"We've built a legitimate business for you three to inherit, not our history of violence."

After dinner and the conversation, everybody retreated to their spaces. Black and Shy were in the media room. The television was on, but they weren't watching. Mr. and Mrs. I'll Kill a Muthafucka had continued the conversation from dinner.

"What else did he say?"

"That every time he comes to the office, I'm sitting there bored out of out my mind."

Shy giggled. "How many times have you come to my office and told me that?"

"A lot. Meka and Gladys run the business. Most days, I'm just there waiting for the next meeting, or I'm in your office, hanging out with you."

"Reeva runs my business. I couldn't move left or right without Reeva," Shy admitted.

"What does that say about what we're doing?"

"That we need to think seriously about what we're doing," Shy said as the doorbell rang. "Maybe we need to find something that you and I could do together, you know, something we both could get into."

"I like the sound of that. A job where I can spend all day loving you."

"That does sound good, doesn't it?"

"We'll figure it out," Black said and took Shy's hand in his.

She squeezed his hand. "We always do."

Chapter Seventeen

Suddenly the door burst open, and Easy came into the media room. "Uncle Bobby is here," he said and sat down. A few seconds later, Michelle came into the room with Bobby, and then she sat down too.

"There they are, Ward and June Cleaver," Bobby said and sat down.

"Who is that, Uncle Bobby?" Easy asked.

"Way before your time, youngster," Bobby said, and then he looked to Easy and then Michelle. "What are you two doing in here anyway?"

"We talked about what you said to Michael over dinner," Shy said.

"You did?"

"I guess they want to see what else you have to say," Shy said.

"Did they really call Daddy Vicious Black, Uncle Bobby?" Easy wanted to know.

"They did, but it was just a name. Anytime somebody got killed, they'd blame it on your father." Bobby laughed. "Even when he was out of the country for six months, if somebody got killed, Vicious Black did it." Bobby pointed at Black.

"So it was all hype?" Easy said, sounding a little disappointed.

"Not all hype, youngster. Me and your father were bad boys in our day."

"But that's behind us now, right, Bob?"

"Until something happens." Bobby paused when he saw the stern looks on Black's and Shy's faces. Then he looked at Michelle and Easy. "What you have to understand is that your father will do whatever he has to do to protect his family. Do you understand what I'm telling you?"

"Yes, Uncle Bobby, we understand," Michelle said, nodding, and Easy shook his head because he didn't quite get it.

"It means that I will never let anything happen to any of you, and neither will your mother."

"You understand that your father and I love both of you very much and that's why we do what we do sometimes?"

"I understand you're only Vicious Black when you have to be," Easy said.

"He's got it," Bobby said.

"Do you really understand, Easy? I did things and do things so you never have to."

"I get it, Daddy," he said, got up, and started for the door. When he did, Michelle got up and followed him out.

"You know you scared them all to death calling yourself Vicious Black Jr."

"I know," Easy said and chuckled.

Michelle stopped and grabbed her younger brother by the shoulders. "Never say that out loud again."

"I won't."

She shook him lightly. "Give me your word, Easy."

"You have my word, Michelle," Easy told his sister.

Michelle pointed in his face. "I mean it, Easy," she said, and they went upstairs.

Back inside the media room, Bobby was shaking his head in disbelief. "Ward, June. I just can't believe the two of you."

"I was a little surprised too," Shy said, nodding.

"We can't keep who we are from them. Look how well that worked out for Barbara."

"Point taken," Bobby said.

Black laughed, and then he turned to Shy. "RJ may have his name, but Barbara is Bobby Ray Jr."

"What's going on with Barbara now?"

"She was having a problem with some gangbangers trying to shake her down for protection money. You wanna know how she handled it?"

"How'd she handle it?"

"She invited them to a meeting, and she killed them."

Shy laughed. "Sounds like you, Bobby." But on the inside, she cringed because Michelle looked up to Barbara.

"Yeah, I know. That's why I'm glad that Brenda and Bonita decided to go to college."

That happened because Barbara scared them straight. They saw firsthand how drinking, smoking weed, and hanging out in all the wrong places led to their sister getting kidnapped. If it weren't for Tahanee showing up just in time to save her, there was no telling what would have happened to Barbara. She could have been raped and murdered, and that was not the path for the twins. Brenda and Bonita decided that they needed to get as far away as they could from The Family their father was a charter member of, and they moved to Los Angeles. Brenda chose to go to UCLA, and Bonita chose USC. They were both currently living normal lives in on-campus housing and without bodyguards.

Bobby stood up. "You in for the evening?"

He thought about calling Rain and telling her to come by so they could talk. "I am."

Shy shook her head. "No, you go on out with Bobby. I need to talk to our children." *Especially Michelle, who thinks her cousin Barbara is so awesome.* "I need to make sure that they really understand."

"I guess we're out then," Black said, and once he was ready, he kissed Shy, and they left the house. As soon as he got in the car with Bobby, Black took out his phone and made a call.

"This Rain."

"Where are you?"

"At the office with Monika."

"Stay there. I'm on my way," Black said and ended the call.

"What did he say?" Monika asked.

"He's on his way."

"Good. Because this shit is getting out of control. He needs to take the handcuffs off so I can start taking it to these muthafuckas," Monika said.

"No, we don't," Rain said and shook her head. Even though there was a part of her that agreed with Monika that they should go hard at them, Rain had responsibilities to The Family. "We need to shut this shit down and get them back their shit so we can get back to doing what's important."

Monika shook her head. "You used to be more fun, sunshine. Now you sound like Black."

"I'll take that as a compliment."

"It was meant to be one," Monika said, and she took a breath. "But I think we need to use that data and make a plan to shut these muthafuckas down just in case they get their shit back and keep coming."

"Agreed," Rain said, and they got with Carla to begin working on a plan.

When Black ended his call with Rain, he made another call.

"Hello."

"Susan?"

"Yes," she answered.

Susan was stretched out across her bed wearing a green Joe Namath throwback jersey and sweats, phone against her shoulder, remote in hand, flipping channels.

"This is Mike Black calling," he said, and Susan turned off the television. "How are you, Susan?"

"I'm doing fine, Mike, and how are you?"

"I'm doing fine, Susan. I was wondering if you were at home this evening," Black said, and Susan sat up in bed.

"Yes."

"Would it be all right if I stop by? I have a question that I need to ask you."

"I'm not doing anything, Mike." Susan got out of bed. "Feel free to stop by anytime."

"I'll see you in about an hour." Black ended the call, and Susan went to the bathroom to take a shower.

However, when Black and Bobby arrived at Susan's house and Wesley let them in, they found that they weren't the only ones who wanted to talk to Susan that night. She stood up when he and Bobby came into the living room. Susan had replaced her Joe Namath throwback sweats with a colorful Josie Natori silk floral caftan and robe.

"Hi, Mike."

"Good evening, Susan. I didn't know that you had company."

"We just stopped by, Mr. Black," Diane said and stood up, smiling. She and Jack had arrived just before they did. "I didn't know Mrs. Beason was expecting you." But it did confirm her suspicion that Susan dressed for the men who came to the house to see her. "And you must be the famous Bobby Ray."

"I am. Good to finally meet you, Detective Mitchell."

"The honor is all mine. Carmen has told me so much about you."

"I'm afraid to say that it is probably all true. But in my defense, I was a younger man those days."

"And I suppose you're a changed man now?"

"He is," both Black and Jack said at the same time.

Diane looked at the frown on Susan's face. *You got all dressed up, and here I am stealing all of your attention,* she thought and gleefully continued. "I stopped by your office to see you this morning."

"Yes, Erykah told me. Did she give you my message?" Black smiled.

"She did, and I gave her my card. I was just waiting on a call back. But now here you are. So is this a good time for us to talk?"

"Of course, Detective." He turned to Susan. "I'm sorry, Susan. We'll have to talk another time."

"Not a problem, Mike. Feel free to drop by anytime. They do," Susan said, and her dislike for Detective Mitchell grew as she escorted them to the door.

"So what did you want to see me about?"

"We wanted to ask you why you thought it was deeper than Gayle and Albert."

Black laughed. "Because Albert is too big a pussy to have killed Elias."

"That's it?" Jack asked.

"Pretty much," he said, unwilling to share what he'd learned. "I guess since you're here talking to Susan, you haven't found Daniel yet."

"No, we haven't." Diane gestured toward Jack. "Susan's got him convinced that she's the innocent, know-nothing wife." She shook her head. "But I think she knows more about what's going on than she's saying."

"I see," Black said, thinking that Diane had good instincts and that they would serve her well. "Have you found Quentin Hunter's killer?"

"Then you don't think Beason did it?" Jack asked.

"No, Jack, I don't. Ebony said that he got there after she did. In my experience, killers don't usually come back after they kill somebody." Black paused. "And I'm sure she told you that he was visibly shaken to see his friend dead. So no, Jack, I don't think Daniel killed Quentin."

"Our lieutenant disagrees," Diane said.

"He thinks Beason came back for something and that was an act for Ms. Maddox's benefit," Jack said, and Black shook his head.

"Why the act? He had just killed Quentin. Why not just kill her?" Neither detective answered. "What do you think?" he asked Diane.

"I agree with you," she said. "I think killing Colton was an accident, but I don't see him as the type to murder his best friend."

Black leaned close to Diane. "With all that's happened, do you still think that Daniel killed Elias, or is it much, much deeper than that?" he whispered to her and walked away.

"What are you trying to say?" Diane asked as Black got in the car with Bobby. He drove off.

Bobby shook his head. "Why are you playing mind games with the cutie detective?" He laughed and then answered his own question. "Because it's fun."

"What did you want me to do? Tell her that she needs to check out an Albanian mafia organization called the Troka Clan and a guy named Lendina Neziri?"

"Wait. Who?"

"Lendina Neziri."

"Who is that?"

"You remember Lendina is the name Wanda got when we went to Tirana. His name is Lendina Neziri. I was going to ask Susan what she knew about him, but that will keep for the time being. In the meantime, I'll get Carla on it."

"So we're going to the office now, right?"

"Unless you got somewhere else you wanna go."

"I was gonna ride by the Four Kings, but that'll keep for the time being."

"What's up with that?"

"RJ said that he and Marvin are working on something they wanna run by you. No big deal. This is much more important."

When Black and Bobby arrived at the office to meet with Rain, she wasn't there. Carla told them about what happened at the hospital and that Rain and Monika got ambushed.

"Are they all right?" Black asked.

"They're fine, Mike." Carla paused. "I'm quoting here: 'There were only four of them.'" Then she told them that they had just left five minutes ago and said they'd be right back."

Black sat down. "What are they doing?" he asked.

"Monika thought that it would be a good idea if we prepare ourselves in case we return their data and they keep coming at us."

"Smart," Bobby said.

"What do you have on a guy named Lendina Neziri? His name has come up a few times in connection to Beason."

"I'll look into it, see what I can find," Carla replied.

"No, Carla. I need you to make finding this guy your priority." Black took a breath. He didn't know anything about Albanian clans or their command structure. "And see if you can find out who's in charge so I can return this data."

"I'll get right on that."

A few seconds later, when Rain and Monika returned to the office, she told Black and Bobby about what happened at the hospital and then about the ambush.

"I think it was the same four guys who hit us," Monika said. "We need to start taking it to these muthafuckas."

"What do you think?" Black asked Rain.

"We need to shut this down and go back to making money," Rain said, and Black nodded.

Chapter Eighteen

"Good afternoon, and welcome to Prestige Capital and Associates. How may I help you today?" Lenecia asked, smiling brightly because it was almost five and she was beyond ready to go.

"I'm here to see Margie Gorman. I have an appointment." She was the vice president of artist development at the Big Night Record label.

"Your name, sir?"

"Scott Lanier with Holloway Promotions."

"If you wouldn't mind having a seat, Mr. Lanier, I will let Ms. Gorman know that you're here," Lenecia said as she watched security come into the lobby to lock the front door. That was her cue to transfer the phone to the night operator. She put on her shoes, got her purse from the drawer, and stood up as Reeva came into the lobby.

"You ready?"

"Almost," Lenecia said as she finished locking up the reception desk as Reeva tapped impatiently on the counter. "Ready," she said, coming around the desk and heading for the door. "Good night," she said to the security guard as he unlocked the door for her and Reeva to leave.

"Where you wanna go?" Reeva asked as they walked to their cars.

"We haven't been to happy hour at Lit Lounge in a while," Lenecia said when she got to her car.

"Sounds good. I'll meet you there," Reeva said and got in her car. The Lit Lounge was a nearby hot spot that they sometimes frequented after work. It was a nice, intimate place with sexy decor, great food, drinks, and music.

They had been there for a little over an hour. They'd had a couple of drinks, and Lenecia was thinking about leaving when she saw somebody they knew.

"Isn't that Richmond?"

"Where?" Reeva asked.

"At the bar, talking to the woman with the purple braids," Lenecia said and discreetly pointed him out at the bar. Reeva looked.

"That's him," she said of Richmond Fox. He was the lead cash disbursement department clerk at the First National Bank. They had gone out a few times six or seven months ago, and she liked him, but then she met somebody she thought she was in love with and stopped taking his calls.

As Lenecia finished her drink, Reeva sipped her drink and watched as the woman with the purple braids, who was sitting next to Richmond, got up and left the lounge. When she left, Richmond finished his drink and turned to look around. That was when he saw Reeva. He smiled and waved excitedly when he recognized her. After they'd gone out a few times, Richmond thought Reeva might be somebody he could get serious about. He had opened up and begun to share his world with her, so he was disappointed when she ghosted him.

"I'm getting ready to get out of here," Lenecia said and reached into her purse to get her credit card. Reeva waved her off.

"I got this." She pulled out her corporate credit card. "I'm gonna hang around for a while," Reeva said, and Lenecia followed her eyes. Richmond waved to Lenecia.

"I see." She got up. "You kids have fun."

"I plan to."

Lenecia left the table, and after stopping to chat with Richmond, she left the Lit Lounge. When she was gone, he got up from the bar and went to the table where Reeva was sitting.

"Hello, Ms. Duckworth."

"Hello, Mr. Fox," she said, smiling. "How are you?"

"I'm great." He pointed at the chair. "Mind if I sit?"

"Please, be my guest," Reeva said graciously and extended her hand toward the chair. "Have a seat."

"Thank you," he said and sat down. "How have you been doing?"

"I've been wonderful."

"It's good to see you, Reeva."

"It's nice to see you too."

"Can I get you another drink, or are you getting ready to leave too?"

"I would love a drink, thank you," she said, and Richmond signaled for a nearby server to take their order.

"I gotta ask," Richmond said when their server left the table, "what happened to you?"

"I could make up a bunch of excuses, but the truth is that I met somebody."

"I thought so." Richmond nodded. "You still seeing him?"

"No, it didn't work out. What about you? You seeing anybody?"

"I'm free at the moment," he answered.

"Maybe we can try it again," Reeva said.

"Promise you won't disappear on me again?"

Reeva leaned forward. "How about I promise to try not to disappear on you again."

"Good enough," Richmond said, and the second act for Reeva and Richmond began.

They hung out there for the rest of the evening and had a nice time together. When it was time to go, they exchanged numbers again before he walked Reeva to her car and Richmond said good night.

When Reeva got home from the Lit Lounge, she was happy that she had reconnected with Richmond. She had kicked off her heels and was about to get undressed when her phone rang. She didn't recognize the phone number, but assuming that it was Richmond calling, Reeva answered.

"Hello," she sang.

"Reeva?"

"Yes, this is Reeva. Who is this?"

"It's Daniel Beason."

"Daniel?" Reeva questioned. "How did you get this number?"

"That's not important now. I need your help, Reeva."

"Look, Daniel, I don't know how you got my number or what made you think that you could call me for help, but I don't want any part of whatever it is you're involved in," Reeva said, and then she hung up.

"Reeva, wait," Beason said, but she was gone. "It was a long shot anyway," he said and moved on to the next number in Colton's contact list.

Beason remembered Reeva Duckworth from the days when she used to work for Colton as a shipping manager at Titanium Distributing Service. He was surprised to see her number still in Colton's contacts after she filed a sexual harassment complaint against him with the human resources department at Titanium, but since it was there, he gave it a shot. He moved on to the next name, hoping that Colton might have given a copy of the data to somebody. What he needed to do was talk to Cissy to see if she had the data or knew where Colton hid it. But that was unlikely. Colton was as adamant about keeping Cissy out of it as he was about Susan's knowledge or involvement in what they were doing. Still, it would be worth a shot.

It was after ten when the phone in the hotel room where he was hiding out rang. Beason looked at the phone. Seeing that he was hiding out, nobody should be calling him.

"Hello."

"We need to meet," Neziri said.

"Neziri? How did you find me?"

"You disappoint me, Daniel. I was sure that when you came back from your visit to Turks and Caicos, I would hear from you. I made assurances to some very important and dangerous people that you would return our property. Now those people are looking very angrily at me. You need to meet me tomorrow at the Red Hook warehouse."

"But I don't have the data."

"Be there at two o'clock," Neziri said, and he ended the call.

"But I don't have the data," Beason said, but Neziri was gone.

He hung up the room phone and picked up his cell. As the phone rang, Beason got up and got ready to get out of that room, wondering how Neziri found him and hoping that Abony would answer the phone.

"Hello, Daniel. Since you're calling this number and you don't have an appointment, I imagine this is important."

"It is. I need a place to crash for a couple of days. Can you help me?"

"I can't imagine why I would want to help you, but yes, Daniel, I can help you."

"Thank you, Abony."

Chapter Nineteen

"What are you getting ready to do now?" Black asked.

"After what happened at the hospital, I moved my aunt. I got her and Sapphire in panic room one at Wanda's safe house. Alwan and Daniella Ramsey are with them."

"Good. Carla said that you and Monika have a plan," Black said as his phone rang. "I need to take this." He swiped to talk. "What's up?"

"Meet me at the Playhouse," Agent McCullough said when he answered.

"What time?"

"As soon as you can."

"I'm on my way," Black said and ended the call. "I gotta go to the Playhouse to meet Mack, see what she can tell me about these guys. But I wanna hear about whatever plans you got."

"Once I make sure they're all right, I'll call you. Monika is with me until this is over, so we'll get with you later, and she can go over her plans."

"Okay." Black paused and thought about whether he wanted to talk to her about Gavin Caldwell, but he decided against it then. "Bobby, we're out."

When Black and Bobby arrived at the Playhouse, he parked across the street. Not only was there a long line to get in, but there were also a bunch of people just hanging around outside. They bypassed the line like they owned the place and walked up to the door.

"Garrett?" Bobby questioned. "What are you doing out here?" he asked because Garrett was one of Barbara's bodyguards, so he generally didn't get too far from her.

"Babysitting." He pointed to the people hanging out in front of the club. "Making sure everybody behaves themselves."

"What we got here?" Black asked.

"The Playhouse is an upscale establishment for adults only. Ladies twenty-one, gentlemen twenty-five." He pointed to the crowd. "Most of these kids can't get in, so they just hang out."

"Reminds me of the old days at the Late Night," Bobby said. Since the Late Night was for members only, those who couldn't get in just hung around outside.

Black chuckled. "It does, doesn't it?"

"Now them niggas over there on the right, that's what's left of the G4Os. They've been losing ground since Rawdawg disappeared."

Bobby smiled proudly. "I heard about that."

"The queen ain't no joke." Garrett paused. "Over there on your left you got the BBKs."

"I heard about them too," Black said and laughed. "Handle your business."

"Always, Mr. Black," Garrett said and opened the door for Black and Bobby to enter.

Once inside, Tahanee told them that Agent McCullough had already arrived and was waiting for them in Barbara's office. Once she apologized for getting them there on short notice and told them that she didn't have much time to talk, she told them that the Albanian mafia was active in Europe, North America, South America, and various other parts of the world. She said they were involved in trafficking drugs, arms, humans, and human organs.

"I know that. What does the FBI have on them?"

"The FBI aren't real big on these guys. They're not serious competition for what the FBI calls traditional organized crime."

"The Italian mob."

"The line I got was that they haven't yet demonstrated the established criminal sophistication of traditional Cosa Nostra organizations."

"You're kidding."

"No, I'm not. Past FBI investigations noted that the Albanian mafia was too widespread and too secretive to penetrate."

"What can you tell me about how they're set up? Who's the boss in New York?"

"That's the thing. There is no single structured hierarchy like the traditional Cosa Nostra. Albanian organized crime groups in this country have a clan structure so there's no one clearly defined boss. The clans are organized around a family or a central leader, and the structure is characterized by strong inner discipline. There are punitive actions for any deviation from internal rules. Since most clans are based on blood relations, the number of clan members are limited, and bonds between them are very strong."

"Damn, Mack. What can you tell us?" Bobby asked.

"That Albanian organized groups are the most violent criminal organizations operating in this country."

"That is not good," Bobby said.

"Sorry, I wish I could tell you more. They were affiliated with some Cosa Nostra crime families before they got strong enough to operate on their own. Maybe your friend might be able to help, but as far as the FBI is concerned, big picture, not serious competition for the old Mafiosi."

"Thanks, Mack. Let me know if you come up with anything I can use," Black said, and Agent McCullough left Barbara's office.

"What are we going to do now?" Bobby asked.

"I don't know, Bob."

"I hate it when you say that."

"What, that I don't know?"

"Yeah, Mike. You're supposed to know."

"What did Mack just say? Sorry, I wish I could tell you more, but I got nothing."

"Might as well have a drink." Bobby stood up and left the office.

Black sat there for a while, thinking. He was the boss of The Family, so yeah, he was supposed to know what to do next. It made him think about Rain. How was she supposed to always make the right decision every time when he didn't always know what to do? He stood up.

"Bobby's right. Might as well have a drink," he said and left the office to join Bobby at the bar.

They had finished their drinks and were about to leave when Barbara came up and stood between them. She put her arms around them and then kissed each one on the cheek.

"What was that for?" her father asked.

"Nothing." She kissed him again. "I love it when you two come to see me, that's all."

"You know I gotta come check on you," Black said.

"He's a little overprotective," Bobby said. "So am I," he said, because although he was proud of her, he worried about Barbara.

"I know, Daddy, but I'll be fine," she laughed, and then she looked at her uncle. "You in a hurry?"

"Not especially. Why?"

"Because there's something I want to show you two."

Bobby stood up. "Lead the way."

As Black tossed some money on the bar, Barbara looked around the Playhouse for Tahanee. When she saw her, Barbara pointed toward the door, and she met her there.

"I'm going to take Daddy and Uncle Mike to see the setup," Barbara said.

"Okay," Tahanee said and opened the door.

Barbara smiled and followed Tahanee out. "I think I'll be safe with them," she said as she walked.

"I'm sure you will be," Tahanee said and kept walking.

"Let the woman do her job," Bobby said.

"That's right, Barbara. Listen to your father," Tahanee said and giggled.

"Whatever, Tahanee," Barbara said and kept walking. Then she pointed to a building across the street. "I'm thinking about renting that space."

"You should think seriously about buying the building," Black suggested.

"I don't have enough money to buy the building yet."

"Talk to your aunt Wanda," Black said.

"That's right, she does own a bank."

"What are you gonna use the space for?" Bobby asked.

"To make that money standing outside the Playhouse. I don't want them in my spot, but I wanna make that moncy."

Bobby laughed because he and Black had done the same thing. "We had a spot down the block from the Late Night."

"The Blue Room," Barbara said.

"Jackie tell you about that too?" Black asked.

"Aunt Wanda," Barbara said, smiling, and it caused Bobby to think.

He and Pam had decided that they would keep his violent world from their girls, so where RJ grew up in The Family, Bobby never told Barbara the truth about the family business, and no one else was permitted to either. Now that his baby girl was aware, he thought that maybe he should be the one to share his world with his daughter as he had his son.

Barbara looked at the two men she admired most and wondered, if she asked them what she wanted to know, would they tell her?

"What's going on with the Albanians?" she asked because everybody in The Family was talking about it.

"We have something they want," Bobby said.

"Why don't you just give it to them?"

Black laughed. "Simple. Why didn't we think of that?"

"We're working on that," Bobby said.

"Who was that woman you met with?" Barbara asked, and Bobby looked at Black.

He kept walking for a while before he said, "If you were any other member of this family, I would tell you that it ain't your fuckin' business. But you're not just any other member of this family." He looked at Tahanee.

"Give us a minute, Tahanee," Barbara said, and she stopped as they kept walking.

"What I tell you, I tell you. Do you understand me, Barbara?"

"I understand," Barbara said calmly, but she was excited.

"That woman is FBI Special Agent Bridgette McCullough."

"So you understand why no one needs to know who she is," Bobby said.

"Yes, Daddy," she said because that was obvious. She signaled for Tahanee, and she rushed to catch up with them as they reached their destination. It was a storefront with the window blacked out. Barbara entered the code on the keypad and opened the door. "This used to be a dry cleaner's."

"I remember," Bobby said as he followed her behind the counter to the rear of the store.

"Welcome to The Family's online gambling operation," she said as they came into the room with racks of com-

puters and a four-person workstation with ten monitors.
Barbara thought that if she could buy the building, she
could move the operation there and would have enough
space to do other things. *Maybe even open that boutique
that Kayla's been bugging me about.*

"Impressive," Bobby said proudly as he and Black
looked around. "Very impressive."

"Thank you, Daddy."

It was at that second that a door opened and LaSean
Douglas came into the room. "Oh," she said, startled by
their presence. "I didn't know anybody was here."

"LaSean, I'd like you to meet my father, Mr. Ray, and
my uncle, Mike Black."

"Nice to meet you, LaSean," Bobby said and shook her
hand, as did Black.

"LaSean is in charge of the operation," Barbara said.

She and Barbara went to high school together and
were reunited at a classmate's wedding. At the time,
LaSean was working on her master's degree in data
science at the New York Institute of Technology. When
LaSean enthusiastically told Barbara about her minor in
data modeling and warehousing and database admin-
istration, and her experience in e-commerce, she knew
that LaSean was the one she needed to set up an online
gambling operation for her.

"What do you think, Uncle Mike?" Barbara asked
because approval was important to her, and not just because he was the boss of The Family.

"I think you're gonna make a lot of money here,
Barbara. I'm proud of you."

"Thank you, Uncle Mike."

Chapter Twenty

"I'm just about done here. You ready to go to the house?" Monika asked.

Rain stood up. "Yeah, I'm ready. But roll me by Romans first. I need to talk to Carter." *Might as well get it over with,* she thought as she got her guns.

It wasn't like she had made up her mind about whether she was going to have the baby or that she had anything to say to Carter. Rain was just tired of avoiding him.

"Let's go," Monika said, and Rain followed her out of the office. Earlier that day, Rain had picked up a new Lexus from Chance that he had customized to hold her arsenal. They had driven a few blocks away from the office when they passed a Volvo with two men in it.

"That's them!" one of the Albanian occupants said.

"Are you sure?"

"Yes, I'm sure. Go after them. But keep your distance. We just want to know where they're going."

"Okay," the driver said and made a U-turn so they could follow Rain and Monika. The other man took out his phone and made a call.

"I have them," he said and gave his location.

The two vehicles converged on Rain's car as they drove, and they were both sure to keep their distance. When they arrived at Romans, Monika parked, and they got out and walked toward the pizzeria.

"Looks like they are going for pizza," one said.

"No matter. Change of plans. We take them here. Now."

All four men armed themselves and got out of their cars. Monika saw them first.

"We got company," Monika said and took out her gun.

Rain looked across the street and saw the four armed men. "These muthafuckas done fucked around and came to the wrong spot." She took out her gun and fired one shot in the air.

Seconds later, Carter, Geno, Chao Hassan, and half a dozen other armed men came rushing out of Romans, firing. As her men engaged the Albanians, Rain went inside Romans and went behind the counter. Monika shrugged her shoulders and followed Rain inside.

"Where's the cook?" Rain looked around. "Never mind." She got a bottle of grape Nehi from the cooler and held it up. "You want one?"

Monika laughed. "Sure, why not?" Rain handed her the bottle. "Thanks. I haven't had one of these in years."

"Want me to throw a slice in for you?"

Monika laughed. "Sure, why not make it two? With sausage and extra cheese. I haven't eaten since breakfast."

Outside Romans, the outgunned Albanians had taken cover. As they fired at Geno, he took cover and fired back at the shooters. He hit one of them with three shots, and he fell over, firing wildly. While two other gunmen continued firing, Carter returned their fire and forced them to better cover.

Chao fired and hit another with three shots to the chest. Carter ducked behind a car and then came up shooting. His shot grazed one's head, and then Carter put two in his chest. The last man came out from his cover, shot back, and then tried to run. He was met by Geno, who killed him before he got very far.

When the shooting stopped, Carter and his men walked across the street.

"Make sure they're all dead, and take them to the Parlor," Carter said, putting away his gun and walking back inside Romans.

When Carter came inside, Monika was leaning on the counter while Rain checked the oven to see if their slices were ready. "Give them another minute," she said and closed the oven.

"Albanians?" Monika asked Carter when he stood next to her.

"I didn't ask, and they didn't say, but I'm sure they were."

"They must have followed us from the office, sunshine."

"I was thinking the same thing," Rain said.

She still hadn't made eye contact with Carter. Even though she had come there intending to talk to him, now she wasn't feeling it. She looked at Carter. "Where are your to-go boxes?"

"Under the prep table," he said and pointed as Geno and Chao came back inside Romans.

All three stood and watched as Rain put together two to-go boxes. Then she got the slices from the oven and boxed them up. She looked at Monika and put the boxes on the counter.

"You want another grape Nehi to ride with?"

"Sure, why not?" Monika said and grabbed the boxes as Rain grabbed two more bottles of grape Nehi.

"We out," Rain said, coming from behind the counter. "Get the door for us, Geno."

"What was that about?" Geno asked when Rain and Monika left Romans.

"I have no fuckin' idea," Carter said, and then he thought, *fuck Rain.* "Buy a round of drinks for everybody on the house, Chao."

Chapter Twenty-one

"Prestige Capital and Associates. How may I direct your call?" Lenecia said as Reeva came through the door the following morning.

She waved as she passed the desk and mouthed, "Talk later," and kept going to her office at CAMB. The call that she received the night before from Daniel Beason still had her shaken. Although she knew him from her days at Titanium, mostly because he used to pester her about having sex with him every time he came into the building to see Colton, there was nothing in that relationship, which consisted of her telling him no, that said, "Call me when you're on the run from the police." Reeva was confused and frightened and needed somebody to talk to.

"Good morning, everybody," Shy said when she came into the office.

Reeva stood up and was at her door when Shy passed. "Morning, Shy."

"Morning, Reeva."

"I need to see you when you get settled."

"Give me ten minutes?"

"Take fifteen."

"See you then," Shy said and continued to her office.

Shy went into her office, put her things down, and stood there. She exhaled. "Coffee," she said, grabbed her cup, and came out of her office.

"You want me to get that for you, Shy?" Elise asked.

"No, thanks, Elise," she said and went to the coffee machine, poured herself a cup, and came back to her office.

When Black got home last night, he told Shy about what Rain and Monika had been going through. Shy thought that she would much rather have been out there trading shots with the Albanians than having the night she had at home. As soon as Black left with Bobby, M and Joanne had come into the media room.

"Why did Michael do that?"

Shy explained to her mother and mother-in-law that Black felt, and she agreed, that they shouldn't hide who and what they were from Michelle and Easy. And after all that they'd been through, they couldn't. The truth was that their father was the head of a criminal organization. Both grandmas said that they understood that. They were more concerned about Easy calling himself Vicious Black Jr. So after spending an hour reassuring the Golden Girls that everything was going to be all right, Shy had gone upstairs to talk to her children. She started with Michelle.

"I'm okay, Mommy. I've known who you and Daddy are all my life, and I haven't lost my mind yet." Michelle had closed the advanced high school statistics book that she was reading. "You don't have to worry about me," she said because she knew her place in The Family. "You need to talk to Easy."

Michelle had gotten up and gone with her mother to her brother's room. With their mother and father being gone and involved in whatever it was they'd been involved in, it usually fell to Michelle to help her brother understand and deal with what was going on. Having established that relationship with her brother made what Shy had to say easier, but it had still taken the rest of the night.

"You ready for me?" Reeva asked, standing in the doorway.

"Come in." Shy waved and Reeva came in, closed the door, and sat down. "What's up?"

"Last night I got a call from Daniel Beason," Reeva said.
Shy sat up straight. "What did he want?"

"He said that he needed my help."

"Help with what?"

"I don't know. I told him that I didn't want to get involved, and I hung up on him." Reeva paused. "What do you think I should do?"

Shy picked up the phone, and Lenecia answered. "Yes, Mrs. Black?"

"Who is in-house counsel this month?"

"Let me check." There was silence on the line while she checked. "His name is Lavonne Reynard."

"If he's in this morning, have him come to my office please."

"Yes, Mrs. Black."

After two police detectives walked into the building and Shy decided that, since she hadn't committed any crimes lately, she would speak with them without having the benefit of counsel present, Patrick Freeman, the head of The Family's law firm, assigned a different criminal attorney to the property so that would never happen again. It was a rotating position because there was nothing to do most days. But every junior lawyer at Wanda Moore and Associates hoped that something would happen during their month and it would be their time to get recognized. Lavonne Reynard was no exception, so he literally ran to Shy's office when he got Lenecia's call.

"Mrs. Black?"

"Yes, Elise?"

"I have Lavonne Reynard to see you."

"Send him in."

After introductions were made, Shy gave him some background on Beason and what he was accused of, and then Reeva told him about the call that she received.

"Let me make sure I understand. You used to work for Elias Colton at Titanium as a shipping clerk, and then you got promoted to shipping manager. That's how you know Beason, and other than that, you have no involvement with him, correct?"

"Yes, that's correct," Reeva said.

"And since you voluntarily terminated your employment at Titanium you've had no contact with Elias Colton?"

"That's correct. I don't even know how Daniel got my number."

Reynard looked at Shy. "I think she needs to be proactive." He turned to Reeva. "Call the police and report the call. Tell them what you told me, and everything should be fine."

"Get Detective Mitchell's number from Erykah," Shy told Reynard, and he quickly got up to get the number from Erykah, overjoyed to be doing something other than playing *Halo: Combat Evolved* all day. He couldn't wait to tell the other lawyers at the firm that not only did he have actual legal work to do, but Mrs. Black herself called him to her office and assigned him the task.

That morning, Jack and Diane were at the precinct when her phone rang. "Prestige Capital and Associates?" Diane questioned excitedly when she looked at her display. "This is Detective Mitchell."

"Good morning, Detective Mitchell. This is Erykah Morgan. I'm sorry to bother you, but do you have time to take a call?"

"Yes, I have time."

"Good. Would you mind holding for a moment?"

"Not at all."

"Hold please."

"What's going on?" Jack asked.

"Erykah Morgan has me holding to take a call."

"Oh, okay," Jack said excitedly because he, like his partner, believed that Mike Black was calling.

"Good morning, Detective Mitchell. My name is Lavonne Reynard. I'm an attorney at Wanda Moore and Associates. Cassandra Black asked me to give you a call in reference to one of her employees receiving a call from Daniel Beason. Mrs. Black was hoping that you would come out to our office and speak with her about the matter."

"We'll be right out, Mr. Reynard. Thank you for calling." Diane ended the call and stood up.

"What?"

"Beason called somebody last night," Diane said, and they left the precinct.

After hanging up with the detective, Lavonne Reynard went to the reception area to talk to Lenecia. "Good morning, Lenecia."

"Morning, Lavonne. What can I do for you?"

"Is there a conference room open this morning?"

"Let me check. Yes, conference room five is available."

"Would you book it for me, please? And when Detective Mitchell and her partner get here, have them escorted there, and let me know when they get here."

"Consider it done."

"Thank you, Lenecia," Reynard said and started for his office.

"Go on, Lavonne, with your bad self. Got something to do," Lenecia said because it had become a running joke, and Reynard hit a step on his way down the hall.

It was a little over an hour later when the detectives arrived at Prestige and were escorted to conference room five, and it was a few minutes later when Lavonne Reynard came in with Reeva Duckworth. Once the introductions were made, Reynard told the detectives the background information of how his client knew their suspect.

"Thank you, Mr. Reynard. Can you tell us what happened, Ms. Duckworth?" Jack asked.

"When I came home last night, I got a call from Daniel Beason," Reeva said.

"What time was it?"

"It was about eleven thirty."

"What did he want?" Jack asked.

"He said that he needed my help."

"What kind of help?"

"I didn't give him a chance to say. I told him that I didn't want to get involved, and I hung up."

"Can I see your phone please, Ms. Duckworth?" Diane asked.

Reeva unlocked her phone and handed it to the detective. While Jack continued to ask questions, Diane looked at Reeva's call list, noted the number and the time of Beason's call, and then she scrolled through the rest of her calls, text messages, and emails before she handed the phone back to Reeva.

"If he reaches out to you again, please give us a call right away."

Jack handed Reeva a card, and then he and Diane headed back to the precinct. The call was made from a burner, and it wasn't on, so that was a dead end. A quick check of Reeva Duckworth's phone and email records showed that she had no connection with any of the parties associated with the case.

"So why would he call her?" Diane asked.

"Desperate?"

Diane shook her head. "No, Jack. You don't call someone you barely know and ask them for help." She paused to think.

"It's deeper than that. Is that what you were going to say?"

"No, I wasn't going to say that, but it is deeper than that. I was going to say that he called her for a reason. Her relationship was with Colton."

"So whatever he wanted her help with had to have something to do with Colton. But what?"

"Add that to the list of unanswered questions," Diane said as her phone rang. "This is Detective Mitchell." Jack sat back and watched his partner nodding and smiling as she wrote something down. Then she stood up, so he stood up too. "Thanks."

"What you got?"

"Andrea Frazier's car was found ten blocks from the warehouse where her body was found."

Chapter Twenty-two

Daniel Beason had lived in New York long enough to know that if you wanted to get around the city and not be noticed, the way to do that was to take the train. Beason got off the train at the Smith–Ninth Streets station and walked to the warehouse to meet Neziri. As he walked, Beason wondered how Neziri found him at the hotel. He seemed to know his every move. Neziri had somebody waiting for him in Turks and Caicos and knew exactly where to find him now that he was back in the country. He thought that he had been so careful, avoiding cameras, paying cash for everything, staying in cheap hotels, and Neziri still found him.

"Not the police, Neziri," Beason said aloud. "Maybe he put a tracking device on you."

But it didn't take him long to figure out that the truth was much simpler than that. Beason had told Neziri that he was going to Turks and Caicos to look for a backup copy.

"Right before he shot Andrea in the head."

Neziri sent two men to Turks and Caicos: the one Marva killed, and the one who followed him back to the country and to the hotel he was hiding out in.

Having solved that puzzle, he continued on his way when a new question occurred to him. *Why?* If he didn't have the drive, why did Neziri want to meet? The idea that he was going there to be killed crossed his mind, and that made him stop to think.

He started walking again when he thought that if Neziri wanted to kill him, he could have done that at the hotel, and no one would have found his body for days. That thought was, but at the same time wasn't, reassuring, but he kept walking anyway because he couldn't see another option.

"I can still fix this, and everybody can go back to doing business as usual."

When he got close enough to see the warehouse, Beason looked and didn't see any cars outside. He thought about waiting until Neziri got there before he went inside, but what would be the point in that? He had no cards to play, so he went inside.

Beason had only taken a few steps past the rows of empty shelves, pallets, and fifty-gallon drums when he saw it: the pool of dried blood and the chalk outline of Andrea's body.

"I'm so sorry, Andrea," Beason said as a feeling of guilt and remorse washed over him.

He stood there, staring at the outline, thinking about Andrea and Quentin, and Beason thought again about calling the police. He had witnessed Neziri kill Colton, and then he stood by helplessly when he killed Andrea in that very spot. There was no reason for him to believe that it wasn't Neziri who killed Quentin. Who else would be at his house?

Beason reached in his pocket and took out his phone. If he surrendered and cooperated, the police would certainly protect Susan and her family. As he started for the door, Beason turned on the phone and was about to call the police when Neziri came into the warehouse with four other men.

"Sorry to keep you waiting, Daniel." Neziri walked toward Beason and took the phone from him. "Traffic. What are you gonna do?"

Meanwhile, ten blocks away, Jack and Diane arrived on the scene where Andrea Frazier's car was found. The crime scene investigator and evidence recovery technicians were processing the vehicle for any latent fingerprints and were documenting and collecting physical evidence. The steering wheel was swabbed, as were the inside door handles and the seat belt buckles. Photographs were taken of the exterior from each side, each corner, front and rear. Another technician had photographed the interior from the front driver's area, from each side with the doors open, the ignition area, the dash, the glove box, the instrument panel, the rear seat area, and the trunk area.

"Anything we can use?" Diane asked.

"Nothing I can see that jumped out at me. We'll check cameras in the area, and I got officers knocking on doors, but so far, nothing. One day it was just there, is what one guy told me. Since we know where the murder was committed, my guess, this is just where they dropped the car."

"I think you're right," Jack said and shook his hand. "Thanks, Sergeant."

"I'll give you a call if we get anything."

"We'd appreciate it," Diane said, and the detectives walked back to their car.

"What do you think?" Jack asked as his phone rang. He looked at the display. "It's Santiago." He answered, "What's up?"

"Beason's burner just came on."

"Where?"

"At the warehouse where Frazier's body was found."

Jack picked up his pace. "We're ten blocks away. Send backup. We're on our way there now," he said as they got to the car.

"What's going on?" Diane asked and got in.

"Beason's burner just came on at the warehouse where Frazier's body was found."

Back at the warehouse, Beason watched Neziri's men spread out in front of him.

"So why are we here?" Beason asked.

"Do you have the drive?"

"You know that I don't have it. I told you that last night. So why are we here?"

"What about the copy that you said that Colton made? Where is that?"

"I don't know. At this point, I can't even say for sure that there ever was a copy."

"Then tell me what purpose you serve," Neziri said, and his men raised their weapons.

"Wait." Beason put his hands out in front of him. "Nothing has to change. We can go back to doing business."

Neziri laughed. "What about your legitimate front?"

"You let me worry about that. I still have the ships and the organization in place, and you have cargo that needs to move. We can make this work."

Neziri nodded because Beason did have a point. He did have the ships and the organization in place, and he did have cargo that needed to move. However, Neziri had a simple solution.

Kill Beason and take over his ships and his organization.

"Police! Nobody move!" Jack shouted.

Neziri's men turned and began shooting at the detectives.

As Jack and Diane ran for cover behind the drums, Neziri shot at Beason as he ran out of the warehouse as fast as he could. When Jack and Diane returned fire,

Neziri ran in the opposite direction, firing shots at the detectives until he was out of the warehouse. Neziri's men had the detectives seriously outgunned, and their gunfire kept them pinned behind the drums. As the four men continued firing, Diane rose up and fired off a couple of shots before quickly dropping back behind the drums. Neziri's men returned fire. She emptied the clip and was forced to take cover again.

Jack fired a couple of shots. "I'm gonna try to make it over to those pallets," he said as Diane reloaded.

"I'll cover you," Diane said, and she came up firing. When she did, Jack moved out, but the barrage of automatic gunfire sent him back to cover.

One of Neziri's men had worked his way around to the side and fired. Jack fired on him, and the shooter went down. He quickly dropped to reload as shots bounced off the drums. He loaded the clip and opened fire.

Diane looked up and saw a man firing his weapon as he came forward. She raised her weapon and fired three times. Each shot hit him in the chest, and he fell backward to the ground.

"Cover me!" Jack shouted and came out from behind the drums. One of Neziri's men began firing at Jack, hitting him with several shots. Diane watched as the impact took Jack's body off his feet, and he hit the ground hard.

"Jack!" she screamed. She stood up and fired at the man who shot Jack. Diane kept firing until she had emptied that clip. She hit him with multiple shots as she moved forward. Then she slammed in a fresh clip, and she opened fire at the last shooter.

"Police!" the SWAT commander yelled as he and his team entered the warehouse.

Seeing the overwhelming firepower that had entered the warehouse, the last of Neziri's men tried to make it to the exit, firing shots as he ran. Diane stopped, aimed her weapon, and fired twice. Both shots hit him in the back, and Diane quickly ran back to Jack.

"I need an ambulance!" she shouted as she ran.

"Officer down! Repeat, officer down!"

Chapter Twenty-three

When Michelle walked into the office at the Onyx Academy of Higher Learning, she was surprised to see Easy sitting there. She was surprised because Easy was the model student. He never got into any trouble.

"Have a seat, Miss Black. I'll be with you in a minute," the administrator said, and Michelle sat down next to her brother.

"What did you do?" she asked.

"I didn't do anything. They just told me to get my stuff and go to the office."

"Me too."

So they sat there for the next twenty minutes, wondering why they were there. The time allowed their minds to wander. Michelle's first thought was that her mother had, once again, gone Pam Grier. She and Easy had watched *Coffy* and *Foxy Brown* together, so they now understood the reference. So now they were waiting for Chuck to get there so he could take them to board the Cessna for the flight to Freeport. Easy was thinking the same thing, only he thought that his father and uncle had gotten into something and it was Vicious Black time. Therefore, they were both surprised when Reverend Jones's door opened to his office and out walked their father.

"I'm glad we had a chance to discuss that, Mike," the reverend said and shook Black's hand.

"I am too. I only wish that you had come to me sooner."

"The foolish pride of an old man." The two men came from behind the counter. "What is it they used to say? Trying to make a dollar out of fifteen cents."

"Yeah, but you were trying to make fifteen cents cover a dollars' worth of expenses." Black laughed. "It doesn't work that way."

"I don't know about that. I know of a guy who fed thousands on two fish and five loaves of bread."

"Amen, Reverend, but in the meantime, I'm glad to help," Black said to the reverend, and he turned to Michelle and Easy. Black nodded, and they stood up.

"Sorry to keep you two waiting. When I saw your father, I had to talk to him," he said.

"No problem, Reverend Jones," Michelle said.

"I came to check you out early."

In their entire school experience, they had never been checked out of school early. Over the years, it was more likely that they would be picked up late, but never early. As Black shook hands with the reverend, Michelle and Easy grabbed their stuff and happily followed their father out of the office.

"What were you and Reverend Jones talking about?" Michelle asked.

"A little budget shortfall. He had to choose between overhauling the HVAC system or buying tablets with the new version of Windows. So Prestige Capital and Associates will be donating the tablets and the parts for the HVAC system overhaul."

"Is everything all right, Daddy?" Michelle asked as they walked out of the building. Since they never got checked out of school early, she thought that something must be wrong.

"Yeah, everything is fine. I just thought that with everything going on, the three of us needed to talk."

"Where's William?" Easy asked when they got to the Alfa Romeo Stelvio Ti.

Black looked around. "He's around here somewhere," he said as Easy got into the back. He opened the door for Michelle to get in. "I tried to give him the afternoon off so we could talk, but we settled on him giving us some space."

"What's going on, Daddy?" Michelle asked.

"Why do you ask?"

"Why are you making me ask? Why can't you just tell me what's going on, Daddy?"

Black looked at his daughter sitting next to him and then to his son in the rearview. "Because my first thought is always to protect you two."

"But—" Michelle began, but her father cut her off.

"Let me finish." He paused. "But now I have to realize that the two of you, especially you, Michelle, are old enough to understand what's going on and deal with it."

"Did Mommy do something?" Michelle asked.

"And now you and Uncle Bobby gotta go all Vicious Black to save her," Easy said.

"No. Your mother didn't do anything." Black shook his head, but that was how it usually went. "Something is going on, but it's being handled. At this point, it's nothing for the two of you to be concerned with, and when it is, I promise to tell you," Black said, looking at Michelle.

"That's all I've been asking for. For you two to be honest with me," Michelle said.

"And that's why we're talking."

Michelle nodded.

"Now I know your mother talked to you two. You wanna ask me anything?"

"How did you get the name Vicious Black?" Easy quickly asked.

"Me and your Uncle Bobby used to work for a guy named Andre. We were drug enforcers, you know, the kind of goons you see on TV," Black said, and his children laughed. "So this one night, Andre took us to collect from a man who owed him twenty-five thousand dollars." He took a deep breath, regretting that he had opened this door. "Your uncle had beaten him so bad that Andre thought he was dead." But now that it was open, he had to walk through it with them. "I took out my gun, held it to his forehead, and shot him. Andre said, 'You just a vicious muthafucka, a vicious black-wearing muthafucka,' and the name stuck."

"Wow," was all Michelle could say.

"How old were you?" an excited Easy wanted to know.

"Not much older than your sister." Black stopped at the light and put the Stelvio in park. "Why don't you drive?" he said and switched places with Michelle so he could concentrate on talking to Easy.

"Where you wanna go, Daddy?"

"Keep driving, and I'll tell you where to go." He turned back to Easy. "But I never liked the name. But like your uncle said, anytime somebody got killed, they'd blame it on me."

"What happened that you were out of the country for six months?" Michelle asked, and Black paused to think of how much of his pain he wanted to share with his children.

"Vickie died."

"Who's Vickie?" Easy asked.

"Somebody Daddy, Aunt Wanda, and Uncle Bobby grew up with," Michelle said as her father paused to reflect on the loss of his friend. One year, on the anniversary of the day that Vickie overdosed in his apartment, Michelle noticed how withdrawn he was, and she asked her aunt Wanda what was wrong with her father.

"Go ahead and tell him."

"She died of an overdose in Daddy's apartment," Michelle said of the moment that changed everything in his world.

"After she died, I killed a few drug dealers instead of collecting from them. That is the world that I came up in. The world your mother and I have tried to keep you two from. But it was always a world we wanted to get out of. Turn left here."

"Where are we going?" Easy asked.

"I wanna show you something. Everything that we did, we did to try to make things better, for us to do better. But even back then, your aunt Wanda saw the future was for us to be completely legitimate. Pull over and park where you can." When Michelle pulled over and double-parked, Black pointed out the window. "That's when we bought that."

"Fat Larry's?" Michelle questioned. "You guys owned a Fat Larry's?"

"We own the franchise," he surprised his children by saying. "That is the first one. You can drive on." Michelle put the SUV into drive and drove on. "That was the first business we bought."

"I thought you owned the Late Night?" Easy asked because he was RJ's partner at the Late Night.

"We rented that space. It wasn't until years later that we bought all the buildings on the block. But my point is that we have always been moving away from what we were to what we are now. After that, she started looking for other legitimate businesses to buy." He thought it best that, for the purposes of this conversation, he leave out that it was to launder the money they were making—a skill their aunt Wanda excelled at. "We bought an insurance company, and then we bought a finance company, and we opened those." Black pointed out his window as they passed a Fast Cash location.

"We own Fast Cash, too?" Michelle asked, and her father nodded.

"We tried to bring services to the neighborhood that it needed. We bought and renovated buildings for people to live in. Yeah," Black said passionately, "we did what we did, and we made a lot of money doing it, but we tried to do some good, too."

"We understand, Daddy," Easy said.

"Do you really?"

"He understands that he should never say he's Vicious Black Jr. in front of Mommy or either Grandma M or Grandma Jo ever again," Michelle said, smiling. "That is what all this is about, right? Mommy and the Golden Girls beating up on you?"

Black laughed. "Take us home, girl."

"I knew it. I saw how defeated Mommy looked when she came dragging in my room after she talked to them." Michelle laughed and headed for home. "I can only imagine the guilt trip that grandma M laid on you."

"Just drive, girl," Black told Michelle, and she drove them home.

She was glad that they had that talk, but to her, it wasn't necessary. Michelle and her younger brother knew exactly who their parents were, and more importantly, she made sure that she and Easy knew who they were. Their parents were king and queen of an empire. Her brother was the prince of The Family, and she was the princess who would be queen of it all. Michelle was happy that her father was inviting her back into his world, and she was ready to take her place at his side. Confident in her position, Michelle got on the highway as her father's phone rang.

"What's up?" Black asked, and Michelle watched the smile that was on her father's face disappear. "I'm on my way."

Chapter Twenty-four

It had not been a good day for Rain. She spent a good bit of it in the bathroom, regretting her decision to have pepperoni pizza the night before despite Daniella's advice to stay away from greasy and spicy foods.

"Mind if I ask you a question, sunshine?" Monika asked when Rain rejoined her in the living room at Wanda's safe house.

"What's that?"

"What's up with you and Carter?"

"What you mean?"

"I mean, you said we were going to Romans so you could talk to Carter, but when you see him, you got nothing to say to him."

"It's nothing. Me and him just got an issue we need to work out, that's all," Rain said.

Monika thought, *bullshit!* "Okay," Monika said instead.

"You think they know about this place?" Rain asked more to change the subject.

"I don't know." Monika stood up. "I know you need to work out whatever it is that's going on between you and Carter. This ain't the time for no foolishness." Monika walked out of the room and left Rain alone.

Foolishness? My feelings aren't foolishness.

Since she didn't want to talk to Carter, Rain got up and went to check on Aunt Priscilla. She was asleep, as was Sapphire. And who could blame them? There wasn't much to do at the safe house. So Rain went and lay down too.

As she lay there, she thought about what Monika said and knew that she was right. Suddenly she felt like her avoidance of Carter was childish, but it was how she felt. She was the boss of The Family, so despite how she felt, and she wasn't feeling it at all, Rain had to put that aside because they were at war. A war that she started. She picked up her phone and called Carter. The phone rang and rang and eventually went to voicemail.

"Now the nigga don't wanna answer."

And he wasn't going to answer. Carter had accepted that Rain was done with him and had said fuck her, and that was it. As far as Carter was concerned, he had done everything that he could do to be understanding that Rain was pregnant, and he had tried to be there for her, but that was over with. *Fuck her.* Rain embarrassing him in his spot the night before was more than he was willing to put up with.

Shedasia Latimer was a big-time basketball fan. She liked the Knicks, but the Trailblazers were her favorite team, and she liked to do her gambling at Romans. She started going there because the pizza was good and there were always good-looking men hanging around. She'd get a couple of slices to go on her way home from work every once and a while until one night she was out late and stopped by while the games were on. Shedasia stayed and watched the game, and that was when she found that she could bet on her Blazers. She was hooked and had been coming to Romans to watch the games and gamble ever since.

Shedasia was there the night before and dove under a table when Rain fired her shot in the air. Then she stayed there with her hands covering her head while the shooting continued outside. Then it stopped, and like everybody else, Shedasia picked up her chair and went back to watching the game. A few minutes later, Chao announced free drinks on the house, and it was as if the shooting never happened. When the game was over, and Shedasia had collected her winnings, she was on her way home when she saw Carter at the bar.

She'd always thought that Carter was fine ever since he got out of jail and started coming to Romans. But the word on Carter Garrison was that he was in love with Mileena, and to her, that made him off-limits. But she could look. While she was watching the game, Shedasia had been watching him drink all night and had seen the look on his face.

"You all right, Carter?"

"No." Carter had turned to Shedasia and smiled. *She ain't a bad-looking woman, and she does have a nice body,* he thought. "But I will be all right. You outta here for the night, Shedasia?"

"My boys made me proud, and they made me some money, so I'm gone."

"Let me walk you home," Carter had said and extended his hand toward the door.

So that afternoon when Rain called, Carter was still at Shedasia's apartment. She had taken the day off from work. Therefore, when his phone rang, his tongue was relishing her rock-hard nipples as if they were candy. Her thighs were parted, Carter was lodged deep inside her, and she was pushing her hips back at him, begging him to fuck her harder.

He flipped her over so her ass was in the air. Carter smacked it once before giving it to her hard. His pumps were swift and had her throwing her ass back to him, her cheeks clapping as he pounded away. Shedasia loved it, and she came, shouting, shuddering, and groaning out his name.

Carter got out of bed and picked up his phone. "Now she wants to talk," he said, walking to the bathroom.

When he had showered and dressed, he came out of the bathroom. Shedasia was still out. He kissed her on the cheek. "See you next time," he said and left her apartment. It took a minute or two before she had composed herself enough to realize that Carter was gone.

When he got outside, he returned Rain's call. "You called me?"

"You wanted to talk, so let's talk," Rain said.

"What do you want me to say, Rain? I don't even know what's going on with you anymore. The only thing that I know is that you aren't talking to me, and I don't know why."

"We're talking now, right?"

"Right. So how are you, Rain?' Carter asked as he walked back to Romans.

"I'm okay."

"Are you someplace safe?"

"Yes. Monika is with me."

"Good, then you are safer than any person in the world. How are you feeling?"

"Stop it."

"Stop what? We're talking, aren't we?"

"Stop fuckin' around. You know what I mean."

"You're the one who needs to stop fuckin' around and talk to me!"

"And you need to stop fuckin' around and tell me about Fantasy!"

"You wanna talk about Fantasy? Fine. I saw her at the fight party, and I fucked her before she went on her secret mission for Wanda. Happy now?"

"No, I'm not happy! Why did you fuck her?"

"Why do you care? You were done with me, Rain. What did you think I was gonna do, sit around and wait until you decided that you were gonna speak to me again?" Which was, until the night before, what he was doing.

"No, Rain. It was never like that between us. How many times did you tell me we were just fuckin'?"

Rain was quiet. "So I'm just trippin', huh?"

"I'm not saying you're trippin', Rain. I just wanna know if you're gonna have the baby."

"I don't know. When I decide, you'll be the first to know," Rain said and ended the call. The phone was still in her hand when it rang again. "What!" she shouted, sure it was Carter, but it wasn't. "When did this happen?" Rain picked up her vest. "I'm on my way," she said, putting on her vest and picking up her guns on the way out of her room. "Monika!"

"What's up?"

"Gear up. We need to go."

Chapter Twenty-five

Although they had the fire under control, fire rescue units and the police were still on the scene at Shooters when Michelle parked the Alfa Romeo down the street. Black looked at his children. He had thought about telling Michelle to drop him off and to go home with her brother.

"Come on," he said, knowing that his wife and the Golden Girls would have preferred that they stay in the car. And if they weren't having the conversation that they were having, maybe he would have done just that, but he didn't, and now Michelle and Easy were walking slightly behind their father to a fire at one of his semi-legal businesses.

For all her big talk about knowing her place in The Family and her one day taking her rightful place as queen of it, Daddy's little soldier had really never been anywhere, nor had she even come close to doing anything. Although she had always known who and what her father was, she was more of a pampered princess than Barbara ever was. Michelle had grown up in the safe and secure environment that her father created to keep her mother out of harm's way in the Bahamas. She was just now getting her first taste of life when her mother took the keys to her car.

As for Easy, he was trying to be cool and keep up with his father, but his eyes were wide open with excitement. Where Michelle was permitted to be in the room while her father conducted business, all that changed when

Shy returned. Therefore, Easy didn't have the insight into The Family that Michelle had. Before that night over dinner, he had only seen The Family through his sister's eyes, so the little prince was even more sheltered from this world than his sister was.

The scene was chaotic, with police cars, ambulances, fire trucks, and half-dressed women in heels walking around the street. Black kept his children behind the police barricades while he looked around for someone he knew, but there was nobody. Knowing that they were just slowing him down, Black looked at Michelle.

"Take your brother home."

"Yes, Daddy. Come on, Easy," Michelle said to her brother.

They made their way back to where she parked the Alfa Romeo and left the scene, each vowing that they would never say a word about them being there. Black stayed behind the police barricade until he saw Michelle drive away before he crossed and went looking for information. By the time he saw somebody he knew, Black knew from listening as he walked through the crowd that the firemen believed that the fire was set. He tapped him on the shoulder.

"Your name is Horne, right?"

"Yeah, who's asking?" He turned slowly, and his eyes opened wide.

"I am."

"Yes, Mr. Black."

"What happened?"

"Somebody set the dumpster out back on fire. It burned through the wall into the back of the club. The fire was blazing, and the club started filling up with smoke by the time anybody really noticed."

"Anybody get hurt?" Black asked as some of the dancers began gathering around him and Horne.

"Everybody got out and nobody was hurt, but some of the girls and a couple of customers had to go to the hospital for smoke inhalation, but that's all. We're just waiting to see if they're gonna let us back in the building to get what's left of our stuff."

"Send everybody home." When he said that, Black looked around at the dancers and saw how they were looking at him. "Everybody's still getting paid, and I'll cover whatever they lost in there."

"Who is you?" one of the dancers asked with an attitude.

"Shut up. That is Mike Black," another said. Black nodded to acknowledge her and smiled.

"And anybody who still wants to work today needs to go to Dime Piece."

"Yes, sir, Mr. Black," Horne said as Black walked away, and the dancers gathered around him.

As Horne began to move the dancers out of the street and away from the building, Black saw Carter's car pull up. He stood there and waited for him.

"What's up, Mike? What happened here?" Carter asked, and while Black explained, Rain arrived with Monika.

"You need to call Chee-Chee and tell her that I sent the dancers there. Tell her to keep whoever she wants, and then you split the rest to the other spots until we can reopen this place," Black said as Rain walked up with Monika.

"What happened?" Rain asked.

"Somebody set the dumpster out back on fire, and it burned into the back of the club," Carter told Rain. As far as he was concerned, he had said what he had to say to her and he was done with it, and her.

"You think it was the Albanians?" she asked.

"I'm sure of it," Carter said.

Black looked at Monika. "They weren't all sophisticated like you two, but they cleared the club out and set it on fire. Retaliation," he said and started walking.

"Where are you going?" Rain asked.

"Around back," he said. "Monika, you're with me."

"Yes, sir," she said, saluted, and followed him around back.

Rain looked at Carter, and then he walked away to follow Black and Monika behind the building before she could say what she was going to say.

"What do you think, Monika?" Black asked once they got to the back of Shooters, where the fire was set.

She looked at the burnt-out dumpster through the scope of Rain's Barrett M82 sniper rifle and what remained of the wall. "Whatever they used burned hot and fast."

"It wasn't a bomb though, was it?" Carter asked.

"No, not a bomb," Monika said. "I'll be able to tell you more when I can get closer."

"Don't worry about that. We know it was arson, and we know who did it."

"What do you wanna do now?" Rain asked.

"I'm going to reach out to Angelo to see if he can't tell me something about who the fuck these guys are so we can return the data to them. But I'm gonna use it to find out who killed Quentin and why." Black walked away. Monika looked at Rain, and then she followed Black.

Rain looked at Carter.

"What?" he asked.

"I'm sorry."

Rain walked away.

Carter shook his head. "Must be something in the water they drink."

And then he followed them back around to the front of the building.

Chapter Twenty-six

Detective Mitchell sat alone in the chapel at the hospital waiting for news about Jack. It wasn't that she was a religious person, far from it, but the chapel was the only place where she would be left alone. For her own sanity, Diane needed to escape hearing and saying the same things over and over again:

"Any news?"

"No, he's still in surgery."

"Sorry about your partner."

"Thanks."

"Glad backup arrived when it did."

"Not soon enough for Jack."

"Jack's a fighter. He'll pull through."

"I know he will."

And of course, there was, "We're all praying for Jack."

Although she understood that these were Jack's friends and it all came from a place of concern for him, it was all too much for Diane, and she had to get away.

So she said a prayer. Made a promise to do better and come to church more often and offered to make any deal she could if God would intervene and save Jack's life. He had been shot five times in the chest and abdomen. One of the bullets had punctured his lung, and he'd been in surgery for the past six hours. By going through tubes placed down the throat into the bronchial airways, the surgeons placed a tube to remove excess air, suctioned out any blood cells and other fluids in the space, and worked to repair the injury. When Diane was permitted to see him in the intensive care unit, Jack was on a respirator, and a chest tube was placed through the ribs into the area surrounding the lungs to help drain the air. She couldn't stand to see her partner like that and rushed out of the unit.

"Where are you going, Diane?" her lieutenant asked as he rushed to catch up with her.

"Back to work."

"No, Diane."

She stopped.

"Why don't you go home and get some rest?"

"You're benching me, aren't you?"

"Major Case is taking the lead on this now."

"It's my case!"

He exhaled and stepped closer to her. "You're too close to this, Diane. I know that you and Jack were more than just partners. I need you to turn over everything you have on the Colton investigation to Major Case, Detective Grandon, first thing tomorrow."

"This is so fucked up," she said as other cops gathered around her for support. "It's my case!"

"I know, Diane. All of us want to get these guys, and we will. I promise you that, Diane. But for now, I need you to stand down and go home, and I'll see you in the morning," the lieutenant said.

"Yes, sir."

Diane walked away from there knowing that she was about to disobey a direct order. She had no intention of standing down, and she wasn't going home. The detective walked out of the hospital and took out her phone. She went to her image gallery, selected and then enlarged an image, and then made a call.

"Hey, Diane. I'm sorry about Jack."

"Thanks, Marita," Diane said and got into her car.

"Anything you need, you just gotta ask, okay?" she said sympathetically.

"I need you to run a plate on a Nissan Frontier for me."

"Give me a second while I get a pen that writes. Okay, give it to me," Marita said and wrote down the number. "I got it. I'll give you a call when I get something."

"Thanks. How's your thing going?"

"I'm following up on something right now. But if it turns out to be like the last one, this source might be the real thing."

"Let's hope it does."

"Diane."

"Yes?"

"I know you're going after these guys, and I meant what I said. Anything you need, anything at all, I got your back."

"Thanks, Marita," Diane said, knowing that she was going off the reservation, and she wasn't about to take anybody down that road with her. "Call me when you get something."

The detective started her car and drove back to the crime scene, to the warehouse where Jack was shot. When she and Jack had arrived at the warehouse, there were two vehicles parked outside: a Honda CR-V and a Nissan Frontier. Diane took a picture of each license plate before they entered the warehouse. Her natural assumption was that one vehicle belonged to Beason and the other belonged to the man he was talking to when they came in, the man who got away. The man she was looking for.

When they were bringing Jack out on the stretcher to take him to the hospital, Diane noticed that only one of the vehicles, the Nissan Frontier, was gone. Did they leave together? Either way, that was the man Diane was looking for, and that second vehicle was where she planned to start. As Diane expected when she got to the warehouse, the second vehicle had long since been taken to impound, but what surprised her was that there were still technicians at the site. Diane got out and went inside, not really knowing what she was looking for.

"What are you doing here, Diane?" the crime scene sergeant asked.

"I just left the hospital." She shrugged her shoulders innocently. "The car drove me here."

The sergeant nodded. "I get it. How's Jack?"

"He's in intensive care. Doctors say it's up to him now."

"Jack's strong. He'll make it."

Diane nodded. "You got anything?"

The sergeant shook his head. "It's Major Case now, Diane." He paused. "And no, I don't have shit."

"Got anything on the shooters?"

"Come on, Diane. It's Major Case now."

"Come on, Sarge. It's my partner." *And I love him.*

"According to their passports, all four were Albanians."

She nodded. "You mind if I wander around? I promise to be a good girl and not touch anything."

"Gloves," he said and walked away.

Once she had gloved up, Diane walked back to the spot where she and Jack first came into the warehouse and tried to visualize what she saw.

"Beason's back was turned to us," she began. "I could see the five men standing in front of him. Four of them were armed with AK-47s, and the other man, the one who got away, he didn't have his gun out then. They were just talking."

Police! Nobody move!

"Beason ran," Diane said aloud as she walked through it. "The men turned and began shooting at us." She began moving toward the drums where they had taken cover. "The man who got away took out his gun and shot at

Beason when he ran the other way. So they didn't leave together. One of them was on foot." She laughed. "My money's on Beason."

Diane left the warehouse, thinking that if this were still her case, she'd check cameras in the area to see if she could see who left, in what, and which way they went. She thought about who she could call who could tell her. She was about to get in her car when her phone rang.

"Mitchell."

"It's Marita. Nissan Frontier is registered to a Besnik Duka. I'm texting the information to your phone."

"Thanks, Marita."

"You want me to meet you there?" Marita asked excitedly.

"Thanks, Marita. But I got this," Diane said, ended the call, got in her car, and drove to the address that she just received.

When the detective arrived at the address, Diane knocked on the door. When there was no answer, she once again donned gloves before she picked the lock. She took out her gun and flashlight and went inside the apartment. Diane went from room to room looking but was careful not to disturb anything. Her search yielded no results, and she was about to leave the apartment when the door opened, and the lights came on.

"Who are you?" the man asked.

Diane raised her weapon, and he raised his hands. "I'm the one with the gun." She moved quickly toward him and pushed him against the wall. "Who are you, and what are you doing here?"

"My name is Besnik Duka. I live here," he said, and Diane cuffed him.

"Sit down," she said and pushed him on the couch.

"You a cop?"

"Shut up. You own a Nissan Frontier?"

"Yes."

"Where is it?"

"My roommate has it."

"What's his name?"

"Lala Arapi."

"Where is he now?" Diane asked even though she assumed that Arapi was one of the four dead Albanians.

"I don't know. He left early this morning."

"With who?"

"With Lendina."

"Who is that?"

"The man he works for."

"What's his last name?" she asked with her gun pointed at him.

"I don't know his last name!" Duka shouted.

"Stand up and turn around," Diane said, and when he did, she uncuffed him. "Keep your hands up and walk to the wall," she said, still pointing her gun at him while she backed out of the apartment.

Chapter Twenty-seven

"What's up, Mike?"

"I need you to come get me."

"Where you at?"

"I'm at what used to be Shooters."

"Used to be?"

"The muthafuckas burned it down."

Bobby laughed. "I'm on my way."

"It's not funny, Bob," Black said, but he was laughing too

"I know it's not funny." He laughed. "I'll be there in fifteen."

When Black ended the call, he looked at Rain. She was talking to Horne, Carter, and Monika. Instead of going over there and taking control of the situation as he usually would have, he decided to let Rain do her job, and he called Michelle. After stopping at Sharkiesha's house to show the Alfa off to her and Tierra, who her brother had a crush on, she and Easy were almost home, so he stayed on the phone with them until they got there.

"We're not going to say anything about you taking us to Shooters," Michelle said as they turned into the driveway at their home.

"Uh-oh," Easy said.

"What?" Black asked.

"Mommy's home," Michelle informed him.

"And?"

"And I'm driving."

"You're driving my car, not yours. Just tell her something came up and you dropped me off on the corner."

"Okay, Daddy."

"She's still gonna ask you fifty million questions," Easy said.

"Your sister can handle it. Just tell your mother to call me," Black said as he saw Bobby's Jaguar coming. "I gotta go. I love you both."

"Bye, Daddy," Easy said.

"Love you, Daddy. Be safe," Michelle said and turned off the car.

"Always," Black said, and he ended the call. He got into the car with Bobby. "Did you wanna have a look around?" he asked before Bobby drove off.

"For what?" He drove away from Shooters. "I've seen shit burned before. Where we going?"

"To see Angelo."

"I thought you said that he avoided these guys like the plague."

"He does. But Mack said that the Albanians used to have ties to the old guard before they got strong enough. Maybe he could reach out to somebody who knows how to get in touch with these guys."

Now that Angelo was boss of the Curcio family, he no longer operated out of a small social club in Yonkers. Black called ahead so that they were expected, and Bobby drove them out to the house where Big Tony used to live. After his death, his wife, Felìcita, and their daughter, Mirella, moved to Palm Harbor, Florida, and she insisted that the house couldn't be sold and had to stay with family, so now it was Angelo's house.

"Bobby Ray and Mike Black to see Mr. Collette," Bobby said to the man at the gate.

"Go ahead. They're expecting you," he said, and with a nod of his head, the gate opened, and Bobby drove in. When they got to the house and went inside, they surrendered their weapons and were searched as Joey Toscano came into the foyer.

"Mikey! Bobby! How's it going?"

"I'm good, Joey. What about you?" Black shook Joey's hand.

"Things are tense right now, Mikey, but we're good. Come on, the big guy's waiting for you." He shook hands with Bobby, and then he walked off. "What about you, Bobby? I hear it's just you and the wife now. Kids are gone."

"It's like a little slice of heaven, Joey."

"Soon as ours are gone"—Joey clapped his hands—"me and the wife are off to Florida like a shot. Sun and Yankees' spring training for me." He shook his head. "Can't wait."

"Mikey! Bobby!" Angelo got up from his spot on the couch and shook hands with Black and Bobby. "How's it going?"

"I'm good, Angee."

"You both still drinking Rémy?"

"All you got," Bobby said, and once Joey had poured them each a glass of Louis XIII, he left the room.

"Joey says things are tense. What's up with that?" Black asked.

"Some people ain't happy with the change of command, and they're making a little noise about it. Nothing I can't handle."

"I thought we took steps so that wouldn't happen."

Before the commission made Angelo boss in his uncle's place, he and Black killed everyone he thought would contest his ascension to boss of the Curcio family.

"This guy, name's Greco Milanesi. He's Luciano Trentini's cousin. Used to run with the big guy back in the day. Did some work in Vegas, did some Fed time, and now he's out and making noise."

"Like he deserves the spot over you?" Bobby asked.

"Like I don't deserve the spot because I killed Trentini."

"Kill him," was the advice that Black had to offer.

Angelo pointed at Black. "I am going to do just that, Mikey. After everybody sees that I made every effort to accommodate this fuck, I'm going to invite him out here and personally put a bullet in this fuck's head." Angelo shot his drink. "Anyway, Mikey, I know you didn't come here to hear about my problems. What's up with you?"

"What can you tell me about the Albanians?"

"That the muthafuckas are crazy. Why?" Angelo asked, and Black explained the reason he wanted to know. "I see what you mean, Mikey. These guys ain't much on talking. They blindly follow orders. But you need to put a stop to this."

"You know anybody I can talk to?"

"I'll ask around, but honestly, Mikey, most of the guys I know don't fuck with these guys."

"So I keep hearing."

"So let me tell you a story. I don't know how true the story is, but it's the story you get when you ask about these guys. Word is that seven Albanians stormed a Mafioso hangout in Queens, tore the joint apart, and beat the club manager and a couple of made guys bloody to send a message. They were taking over the club."

"Bold move," Black said.

"So they have a sit-down to settle it. They met at a gas station at a rest area on the New Jersey Turnpike. Twenty armed Mafioso soldiers." He paused. "The Albanians, they come with six guys. Words are exchanged, and the Albanians and the Mafioso all pulled out their guns."

"Outnumbered and outgunned," Bobby commented.

"You know what these crazy muthafuckas did?"

"What?"

"The Albanians threatened to blow up the gas station with all of them in it."

Bobby chuckled. "I bet that ended the discussion."

"Both sides backed down," Angelo said.

"Outnumbered and outgunned. I call that resourceful," Black said and finished his drink. "Can you help me?"

"I'll see what I can do, Mikey," Angelo promised, and Black and Bobby headed back uptown.

"Take me to Susan's house," Black said as Bobby drove.

"Not that I mind—she is finer than a muthafucka—but what you wanna go there for?" he asked and headed for her house.

"I wanna ask her if Beason ever mentioned Lendina Neziri to her or if she ever heard him talk about him."

"That's more likely. You heard her. She pays attention to everything for her own protection."

"If I were in her position, I would too." Black laughed. "You need to know what you don't know about when you're talking to the police."

It was getting late. Therefore, Susan's mother, sister, and nephew had all called it a night and had gone up to bed. After straightening up around the pool and the living room, Susan went upstairs thinking that it was time for them to go home. She got undressed and settled into a long, hot bath. While she soaked, Susan thought about her day and the things she'd done to move forward with her life. She had opened new checking and savings accounts and had gotten new credit cards in her name only. Susan had been putting money away for years in accounts in the Cayman Islands, so even if she were forced to settle with Beason's defrauded investors, as Connie Lewis suggested she might be required to, she'd still be all right.

What worried Susan more than the money was if she had any legal exposure. She knew that she needed a lawyer, several when she really thought about it: a criminal lawyer to keep her from going to jail, one to protect her from going broke, and a divorce lawyer to get her out of this mess when it was all over.

As she dressed for bed in a Fleur du Mal orchid silk pajama set, Susan thought that it would be a good idea if she were to gather what were now her financial records. Something else Connie Lewis suggested. She pulled her hair back in a ponytail, thinking that hiring a new accountant would probably be a good idea, too. Susan picked up the embroidered silk wrap robe that matched the pajama set and went downstairs to what was now her office. Susan sat down at the computer and turned it on. She had figured out years ago that his password was her birthday backward, and she had just typed it in when the doorbell rang. She looked at the time.

"Fuckin' cops."

Susan was sick of them showing up at her house at all hours of the night and day. She clicked on the security feed icon for the front door on her desktop and saw that it wasn't the police.

"Mike Black. What is he doing here?" she asked and allowed herself to imagine that he had come there to seduce her until she saw that Bobby was with him. "Doesn't matter. He's here." Susan let her hair loose and went to answer the door. "Hi, Mike."

"Hello, Susan," Black said. "Sorry I didn't call first, but is this a good time for us to talk? Or are the police inside?"

"You never know. They may be here any second." Susan smiled. "Come on in, Mike."

"Thank you, Susan. You remember my friend, Mr. Ray?"

"Yes." Susan nodded at Bobby. "Good to see you again, Mr. Ray," she said as she led them into the living room.

"Good to see you too," Bobby said, admiring Susan as she walked.

"Please have a seat."

"I'm sorry to come by so late, but—" Black began as he and Bobby sat down on the couch across from Susan.

"But I did say to feel free to drop by anytime," she flirted as she sat down. Susan crossed her legs and placed her hands on her lap. "Tell me what I can do for you, Mike."

"Did you ever hear Daniel mention somebody named Lendina Neziri?"

"That's the foreign guy Danny was in the illegal shipping business with who I told you about," she said excitedly. "Now that you mention his name, Lendina, I remember that Danny introduced me to him. I remember because it's not a common name."

"What else do you know about him?"

Susan looked earnestly at Black, inhaled, and let her breath out slowly. "I'm sorry, Mike, but that's all I can tell you about him. I only met him that one time."

"Then you wouldn't know where that was, or how I could get in touch with him?"

Susan sighed deeply. "I'm sorry, I don't know how to get in touch with him," she said, and then she thought about having access to Beason's computer, so soon she would know all his secrets. Susan decided not to share that with him. "But we were at a place called Sunny's Bar when Danny introduced us."

"Where is Sunny's Bar?"

"It's a little bar near Valentino Pier in Brooklyn. But that was years ago, Mike."

"You haven't heard from Danny again, have you, Susan?" Bobby asked.

"No, Mr. Ray." She laughed playfully. "I haven't heard from him." She looked at Black. "If I had, it would have been the first thing I told you."

"I don't know why your husband hasn't reached out to you. I know I would have called a beautiful woman like you," Bobby said.

"Well thank you for noticing," Susan said, and looked at Black. "And for the compliment, Mr. Ray."

Black stood up. "Thank you again, Susan. I think we've taken up enough of your time."

"I just want to be helpful to you," she said and walked them to the door.

"You are, Susan, very helpful."

Susan stopped at the door and opened it. "It was good to see you again, Mr. Ray," she said and shook his hand.

"It was my pleasure."

"Mike." Susan turned to him and held out her hand.

Black took her hand to his lips. "Always good to see you, Susan."

"Likewise," she said breathlessly as Black let go of her hand. Susan quickly composed herself. "There is one thing that I wanted to talk to you about before you go, Mike."

"What's that?"

Susan stepped closer to Black and looked up into his eyes. "I am going to need legal representation to get me through this, and I understand that you own a law firm."

Black reached into his pocket and took out a card. "Just give her a call whenever you're ready."

"Is she your lawyer?"

"No, Erykah is my personal assistant. Just give her a call when you're ready, and she'll take care of you."

Susan smiled and looked at the card. "Thank you, Mike. I really appreciate your help." *And for the access I now have to you.*

"Good night, Susan," Black said and turned to walk away.

"Good night, Mike. Feel free to stop by anytime," Susan said and watched them walk away before she went back inside.

Chapter Twenty-eight

"She is so fuckin' sexy," Bobby said as he drove away from Susan's house.

"I told you, Susan is fine as hell," Black said, shaking his head.

"When she laughed and them titties started bouncing, I—"

"I knew that I needed to get you up outta there before you started telling her jokes."

"Because you know I was just getting started." He laughed. "And it was you who needed to get you up outta there."

"What you mean?" Black asked, but he knew what he meant, and he knew that Bobby was right.

"I've known you as long as I can remember, Mike, and I know you have a type."

"I know that, Bob."

Bobby laughed. "Shit, even Shy knows you have a type, and she knows that Susan is definitely your type."

Susan was his type, and for that reason, she moved him in ways that, to this point in his life, only Shy and Jada had, and that worried him. Although he'd never admit it to Bobby, he was glad that Jada lived in another country, too. Susan wasn't safely tucked away in another country. She lived in Scarsdale, a twenty-five-minute ride from his front door.

"Feel free to stop by anytime, Mike," Bobby said, imitating Susan's sultry voice. "All you gotta do is pay me a little attention and this pussy is yours, Mike," he continued.

"I know that, Bobby," Black said, and then he noticed that Bobby was driving downtown. "Where we going?"

"Tribeca."

"Fuck are you going to Tribeca for?"

"I told you that RJ and Marvin got something that they wanna run by you."

"You know what it is?"

"Yeah, it's something they wanna run by you." Bobby took out his phone.

"Who you calling?"

"Marvin. He said to call him if we can make it by there tonight."

"Tell him that we're on our way."

Black relaxed and they drove to Pesce Tribeca, one of the restaurants that Marvin owned. On the way, Black called Michelle to make sure everything went all right with her and Easy when they got home. She told him that once she told Shy that she dropped him off at Shooters and that he would call her later, she said okay, and that was that. "And I made sure that William was on the same page."

"That's my girl," her father said, and then he had to go.

"Bye, Daddy."

Michelle ended the call, thinking about how much she really liked driving the Alfa Romeo much more than she liked driving her car. The interior was laid: leather upholstery, power-adjustable front seats, heated front and rear seats, and the steering wheel was heated. The Alfa had a dual-pane sunroof, remote push-button start, dual-zone automatic climate control, Bluetooth, four-teen-speaker Harman Kardon stereo, an eight-inch touch screen, and auto navigation. Michelle had decided that when her mother gave back her keys, she would ask

her father if she could drive the Alfa. He only got it because her mother thought it was cute. Since he didn't like
to drive, that would be her car after that.

When Black hung up with Michelle, he called Rain and
told her and Monika to meet him at Pesce Tribeca. He
wanted to hear what they had planned to shut down the
Albanians if they kept coming at them after their data
was returned. As much as he hated it, Black had to consider the possibility that that was exactly what would
happen.

Black and Bobby arrived at Pesce Tribeca, one of the
two upscale restaurants that Marvin owned in Tribeca.
The other, Trikala Greek Taverna, served authentic
Mediterranean cuisine. He also owned a small chain of
three fitness centers called Healthy Lifestyle: the Power
Punch Gym, and Marvin controlled the contract of
welterweight prospect Alex "The Bronx Bomber" Benton.

Although everything seemed wonderful in his world,
Marvin was still dealing with his feelings over the be-
trayal and loss of his relationship with Sataria, a woman
who had killed multiple husbands. Although he really
didn't like how it sounded, by definition that was who
Sataria was: his own personal black widow.

Marvin had never loved a woman the way that he
loved Sataria. She had shattered his trust. The sadness
of the loss of the relationship that he thought that he
was building with her was depressing. Thinking back
about the good times in their relationship only made him
miserable. That was when the thought settled in that he
would never love or completely trust a woman ever again.
However, there was nothing like the comfort of a woman.
The two were inconsistent: wanting the pleasures of
women, but never trusting them.

There was an old saying in player logic that the way to
get over your woman was to fuck another one. The more
women you fucked, the merrier. He had been fucking

Joslin Braxton. She meant it when she said that she was nothing but a drug dealer's girlfriend. And once she realized that Marvin wasn't going to take care of her in the manner she'd become accustomed to and he actually mentioned that she consider getting a job, Joslin moved on. However, she did call every once in a while to get some.

Marvin had begun seeing Savannah Russell. She was the assistant to former IBC middleweight champion turned fight promotor Frank Sparrow. He also had his eye on LaSean Douglas. She was setting up an online gambling operation for Barbara. Each time he saw her, LaSean had made it obvious to him that he could have her with just a bit of effort. So he was working his way around to her, too.

Black and Bobby were greeted by Amy, the hostess at Pesce, and she escorted them to a small private dining room that was off of the main room. When they were seated, Liliana wheeled to the table a cart filled with food samples, a bottle of Rémy Martin Napoleon, a carafe of apple martini, and three glasses. When Black saw the carafe, he knew that Wanda had been invited to hear whatever it was that Marvin and RJ wanted to run by him. While Liliana poured their drinks, Black and Bobby helped themselves to the samples, and it wasn't long before Wanda arrived at Pesce, and Amy escorted her to the dining room. Bobby was surprised to see her when she walked into the private room.

"What are you doing here?" Bobby asked.

"RJ called and asked if I could meet you and Mike here, so here I am." Wanda sat down, and Liliana poured her an apple martini. "Thank you," she said to Liliana. "What are you doing here?"

"RJ said that he and Marvin had something they wanna run by Mike," Bobby said.

"Apparently it's something they want to run by all of us," Black said as Marvin and RJ came into the room.

In addition to being Sherman's top lieutenant, RJ had established himself in the entertainment industry as a producer and as a multi-city concert promoter. Where Marvin had accepted that he would never love a woman again, RJ's problem was the opposite. He was in love with two women: his current girlfriend, Mia Rubio, and his ex-girlfriend Venus.

When Venus gave him an ultimatum, "Marry me or it's over," RJ, who wasn't ready to get married, let her walk away. Heartbroken, RJ threw himself into his work and went on tour with The One, and he tried to forget about Venus in nightly orgies. When he returned from tour, he met *The Breakout* contestant Mia Rubio, and the vibe between them was immediate.

What RJ didn't know was that Venus's plan hadn't changed. She still intended to marry him, and there was something else. Venus was pregnant. Since her plan hadn't changed, while he was on tour Venus kept coming to Sunday dinner with his family and never mentioned that she had broken up with him because he wouldn't marry her. Imagine his surprise when he showed up for Sunday dinner and there was Venus.

They fought about it and had makeup sex over it, and then Venus told RJ that she was pregnant with his baby. He promised to stand by her and be there for his child, but he still wasn't ready to get married. They fought about it and had makeup sex over it, but it changed nothing for him, and Venus angrily ended it again. But Venus still wasn't done. Her next move was to tell Bobby and Pam that she was pregnant, and for Venus, it was the move that turned everything around in her eyes. Before she and Bobby left to go on vacation with Black and Shy, Pam had sat Venus down and had a chat.

"You need to stop being so stupid."

"Excuse me?" Venus had asked Pam indignantly because nobody talked to her like that.

"You need to stop acting like a stupid little girl and start acting like a woman. Stop being so demanding all the time. It gets on my nerves, with you whining about . . . about every little thing, so I'm sure that it gets on his nerves too."

That conversation with Pam had an impact on the expectant mother, and she made changes in her life and how she dealt with RJ.

Now it may or may not have had something to do with what Marvin called "that massive guilt trip" his sister, Tenikka, who had grown up without their father in her life, laid on RJ, but he was totally committed to being there for Venus and his child.

"I need my brother to be a better man than our father was. Can you do that for me?" Tenikka had asked of her brother, and he promised that he would.

Although she was still extremely needy, the new Venus was patient, considerate, and understanding of RJ's time. He noticed the change and the effort that she was making, and RJ, who still loved her, appreciated this new Venus. Since she was no longer any trouble at all, RJ would happily do whatever she asked.

"For the baby."

Therefore, while Mia was on tour in Europe opening for Cristal, Venus had moved into his parents' house, and they were having a baby shower for her at Black and Shy's house.

RJ fist-bumped with Marvin, and he approached the table. "I know you all are busy," Marvin began.

"So we want to thank you for coming tonight," RJ said.

"At Uncle Mike's urging, The Family now has a controlling interest in the Spring Hill Media Group," Marvin said and looked at Black. "As we discussed, RJ and I have expanded his promotion company to include boxing in areas where he has existing relationships."

"Because of Big Night Records and the success of *The Breakout,* we plan to develop music programming," RJ said. "We've been working with Margie Gorman, the vice president of artist development at Big Night, so we have access to a lot of musical talent we're not utilizing. Using those same relationships I've built around the country, in addition to music content programming, competition shows, musical-based reality shows, and documentaries, for example, we'll also have the capacity to produce sports entertainment programming with Spring Hill for distribution."

"We could go into detail about how everything is going to work," Marvin said and held up the proposal they had written. "But what do you think, Uncle Mike?"

"It all sounds good, but since you know I know most of this, what did you need from me?"

"We don't need anything, Uncle Mike. We just want your blessing before we moved forward," RJ said.

"All of your blessings," Marvin added quickly.

"I'm flattered just to be consulted," Wanda said modestly. "I would like to go over the details of your plan with you, but I agree with Mike. It all sounds good." Since she never had any of her own, Bobby's children were her children, so she was proud of what RJ had accomplished and the small part she played in getting him started in the music business.

"What about you, Pop?" RJ asked because it was important to have his father's approval.

"I'm so fuckin' proud of you, son," Bobby said. "That all sounds great, RJ."

"Thank you," both RJ and Marvin said.

"Congratulations," Black said, and he stood up thinking that this was nice. "I'm sure it'll be very successful, and we'll all make a bunch of money."

He appreciated that they thought enough to seek their approval. If this were any other time or under any other set of circumstances, he would have told Marvin to break out the champagne so they could celebrate, but this was not the time. They were fighting a cold war with the Albanians, and there was no time to waste.

"We're out."

Bobby stood up, and he shook hands with RJ. "I'm proud of you," he said and hugged him.

"Thanks, Pop."

"I'm gonna stick around here for a while. I wanna hear more about your plan," Wanda said as Black and Bobby walked toward the door. "Call me tomorrow and let me know what's going on with the Albanians, Mike."

"I will."

Black and Bobby stepped outside as a van came to a screeching stop in front of Pesce Tribeca. When the panel door opened, five men jumped out. Black and Bobby dove for the ground as their Albanian attackers spread out and opened fire on them. As the glass shattered, the customers inside Pesce dove under tables for cover. RJ, Marvin, and Wanda ran to the office to the weapons safe that each location in The Family had. Marvin opened the safe and grabbed two AK-47s. He handed one to RJ, and they ran out of the office. Wanda got a 9 mm and some clips and went to get into the fight.

"You hear that?" Monika asked. She and Rain weren't far away from Pesce to meet Black and Bobby.

"Sounds like shooting," Rain said, and Monika drove faster.

As bullets flew over their heads, Black and Bobby took out their weapons. Marvin and RJ took up positions in the window, and all waited for an opportunity to return fire. When Monika rounded the corner, Rain had already mounted the M203 grenade launcher on her M4 carbine. She opened the sunroof, stood up, and fired.

"Look out!" one of the men yelled.

The explosion that followed took out the van, the driver, and two of their Albanian attackers. RJ stood up and fired, and one man went down. Marvin raised the AK-47 and fired. His shots hit one in the chest, and he fell to the ground. The remaining attacker continued firing, so he was easy prey for Black. He stood up quickly, raised his weapon, and shot the last of the men.

He extended his hand to help Bobby up as Wanda came out of Pesce with RJ and Marvin.

"Everybody all right?" Black said.

"I'm fine," Wanda said, and RJ nodded.

"I'm going to check on my customers," Marvin said and went inside as Rain and Monika walked up.

"Everybody all right?" Rain asked.

"We're okay," Black said and turned to Monika. "You were right. I'm tired of fuckin' around with these mutha-fuckas. It's time to start taking it to these bastards."

Chapter Twenty-nine

First thing in the morning, Diane was back at the hospital checking on Jack. The doctor told her that there was no change in his condition and told her once again that it was all up to Jack now. She thanked the doctor for all he had done to help her partner, and then she left the hospital. When she arrived at the precinct, Diane sat down at her desk and looked across at Jack's empty chair. She shook it off and turned on her computer to run a name: Lendina. What she got back from her search was Lendina Neziri, and she began reviewing his record.

"Mitchell!" the lieutenant shouted from his office.

She got up slowly and walked to his office, not really looking forward to the conversation they were going to have, or about the idea of being closed out of her case. Diane tapped on the door.

"You wanted to see me?"

"Yes, Diane. Come in and have a seat."

Diane looked at the man seated in front of the desk and stepped inside but chose not to have a seat.

"Diane, this is Detective Evan Grandon of the Major Case Squad."

He stood up. "Good to meet you, Detective." He shook Diane's hand. "Sorry about your partner."

"Thank you."

"You know the routine, Diane. Turn over what you got to Detective Grandon and bring him up to speed."

"Yes, sir." Diane saluted and walked out of the office.

Grandon shook his head. "This is gonna be fun," he said and started to follow Diane out.

"He wasn't just her partner, Detective, so maybe you'll think about taking it easy on her."

"Got it," Grandon said to the lieutenant as he left the office.

For the next hour, Diane reviewed with Detective Grandon the case that she and Jack had been working. She shared everything that they had and told him about her suspicions about Susan knowing more than she was saying. Then Diane went into detail about theories they'd had of the crime and how each new lead led them nowhere. Despite her very bad attitude about it, Grandon was surprised at how helpful Diane was.

"That's all I got."

"Thank you, Detective."

Diane stood up. "Catch these guys," she said and started to walk away.

"Mitchell?"

"Yes?"

"You know Detective Eisenberg?"

Diane cracked her first smile of the day. "Yeah, I know Jason. He was my training officer when I hit the streets. How's he doing?"

"He's good. He just got promoted to Major Case. He said to tell you hello."

"You tell him that I said congrats, and tell him that we need to have a drink, on me, to celebrate and catch up."

"Glad you said on you, or the cheap bastard wouldn't show."

Diane laughed and started to walk away again. "That's Jason."

"Detective?"

She stopped. "Yes?"

"We'll get these guys. You have my word. You can't just shoot a cop and get away with it," Grandon said, and as he left the precinct, Diane returned to her lieutenant's office.

"What now? Come in, Diane, and have a seat."

This time she did sit down. "You're not gonna assign me a new partner, are you?"

"No, Diane. But I am putting you back in the rotation. The next case up is yours."

"Yes, sir."

"Where are you on the Menendez case?"

Samantha Menendez had been found shot twice in the chest outside her building. Witnesses reported seeing a black man wearing a dark-colored hoodie running from the area before jumping into a white SUV.

"Nowhere. Do you have any idea how many men in New York match that description?"

"Only one who's important. The killer."

"Yes, sir."

The next case up was the murder of Trena Gellert. She was beaten and then shot by an intruder inside her residence. When Diane arrived on the scene, the first responders informed the detective that witnesses observed one male with blood on his shirt running from the scene after they heard the shot.

"You got a description for me?"

"White male, early twenties, approximately five ten, weighing between one hundred and sixty-five to a hundred and eighty-five pounds, wearing a dark-colored shirt and red knee-length shorts. Last seen on foot heading north," he said and pointed in that direction.

"Got it," Diane said and headed north.

She had walked a couple of blocks when she passed an alley and caught a glimpse of a man sitting on the ground, nodded out on heroin. Diane stopped and walked back, and that was when she saw the tube still tied around his arm.

"White male, early twenties, red shorts, dark-colored shirt with blood on it." She took out her weapon and kicked his foot. "Wake up, asshole. You're under arrest."

With that case closed and the paperwork done, Diane pulled out the Menendez case file and was about to dig in when she had a better idea. She put the folder back in her drawer, grabbed her weapon, and headed out. Her destination: the Major Case Squad. Her objective: Detective Jason Eisenberg.

To have a drink to celebrate and catch up.

"Don't get involved in this, Diane," Eisenberg said when she tried to get information about the Honda CR-V that was impounded from the warehouse.

"If you don't tell me, Jason, I'll just go to the impound yard and find out anyway."

"Geez, Diane," he said and gave her the information.

"Thank you, Jason. I still wanna get a drink and catch up," Diane said on her way out of the Major Case Squad.

The vehicle was registered to Elezi Dushku—deceased, as she expected—but Diane checked his record and got his address, and then she checked for known associates. She found five. Two were in jail on weapons violations, one had been deported back to Kosovo, and that left two who were still on the street: Prifti Shehu and Henricus Kreshnik.

When Diane went to question Shehu, he had moved from his last known address, so the detective moved on to Henricus Kreshnik. His record included arrests for prostitution and arms and drug trafficking.

When Diane arrived at the house, she saw a man matching Kreshnik's description outside the house. He was standing at the door, looking around, frustrated, as if he were waiting for somebody. Kreshnik looked around again, and then he went back inside. The detective put on her gloves before she got out and approached the house. Diane took out her gun, pointed at the door, and then she started banging on it. The door suddenly swung open.

"About time you got here," Kreshnik said, and then he put his hands up when he saw Diane's gun pointed at him.

"Inside," Diane said, motioning with her gun. With his hands raised high, he backed into the house. "I'm looking for Lendina Neziri. Where is he?"

"I don't know what you're talking about. I don't know anybody named Neziri."

"Turn around and face the wall."

Kreshnik turned slowly.

"Hands against the wall."

Once he had his hands against the wall, Diane put her gun to his head and started searching him. "Gun," she said aloud more out of habit and took it from him. She put Kreshnik's gun in her waistband before returning her weapon to his head and continuing to search him.

Diane heard a noise. "What was that?" Diane pressed the gun harder against his head. "Who's here with you?"

Kreshnik said nothing.

"Police! Is anybody here?" she shouted.

"Help us."

It was faint, but she heard it, and Diane made the mistake of relaxing the pressure of the gun against Kreshnik's head. He took advantage of the opportunity. With the detective's attention diverted, he turned quickly, grabbed her wrist, and tried to wrestle the gun away from Diane. As they struggled, Kreshnik's gun dropped on the floor.

He forced Diane to the wall and began banging her hand against the wall until she dropped her gun. Kreshnik grabbed Diane by the throat and began choking her. As she struggled for air, Diane tried to pull his hands from around her neck, but he was too strong. She began bringing her knee up to his groin, over and over as hard as she could, before he let go and threw Diane to the ground near his gun. She grabbed it quickly and pointed it at him.

"Move and I'll kill you!" she shouted, then got to her feet. "Police! Who's in here!"

"Help us, please." This time it was louder, and Diane could tell there was more than one voice.

"Move," she said and put the gun to the back of his head. "Where are they?"

Kreshnik led the detective to the basement door, unlocked it, and led Diane down the stairs. The first thing that hit her was the smell.

"Oh, my God," Diane said when she saw the women locked in cages. There were two cages with ten women in each. Some had torn clothing, and a couple had no shoes. There was no bathroom, just a can. She hit him in the back of the head. "Open them."

The second the cages were unlocked, the women ran out.

"Stop! Wait!" she shouted, but she could do nothing but watch as the women ran up the stairs.

When Kreshnik moved toward her, Diane shot him in the face. Then she took a step forward, stood over his body, and shot him in the chest.

"Bastard."

Not knowing how much time she had before whoever Kreshnik was waiting for or the police got there, Diane went upstairs and searched the house. What she found was an address written on a bar napkin. She drove away thinking about the women she'd released. That was a good thing that she'd done. Diane wondered where they would go and what they would do now that they were free. And then she thought about the address on the bar napkin and hoped it turned out to be something since she killed a man to get it.

Chapter Thirty

Diane's day began the way the previous one ended. She was at the hospital, checking on Jack's condition. His condition wasn't improving. Jack was still in the intensive care unit, breathing through an endotracheal tube. A chest drainage tube was inserted to remove air and fluid from around his lungs, and Jack was receiving fluids to prevent dehydration and increase blood flow to his major organs. She was getting used to seeing him that way, and that bothered Diane too, so she left the hospital and got to work.

She wanted to check out the address that she had gotten the night before. Diane drove away from the hospital thinking about Henricus Kreshnik and how she felt about killing him. No one deserved to die, but then again, Diane couldn't escape the image of the women locked in those cages, how they were forced to live in unsanitary conditions. She couldn't imagine the horrors they had been subjected to or the life of sexual exploitation that awaited them. And then there was Jack, fighting for his life. The more Diane thought about Jack, the less remorse she felt for killing him.

The detective took a minute to think about it and why it happened. Although she didn't go there to kill Kreshnik, Diane did go there looking for Neziri, and she wanted revenge. She wanted revenge, and she was mad enough to kill. Coupling that with the adrenaline rush from the fight and the disgust at seeing those women angered her, and then he'd moved.

"I told him if he moved, I'd kill him," Diane said aloud as she drove.

But there were still questions that she had to answer for herself. Why did she leave the scene? Why didn't she call it in? Diane laughed because she knew that the answer was simple, she just needed to accept it. She shot an unarmed man in the face at point-blank range, and then she stepped up, stood over his body, and shot him in the chest because she was mad enough to kill.

Does that make me a killer?

When Diane arrived at the Fifty-eighth Street address in the Sunset Park section of Brooklyn she'd gotten from the house, she found a warehouse. She got out and tried the door, but it was locked. After her knocks went unanswered, the detective walked around to the side of the building. There were no windows that she could look in, so once she tried the back and found the door padlocked and chained, Diane went back to her car and headed for the precinct. She drove by Kreshnik's house on the way to see if there was any activity, and when she didn't see any, Diane drove on.

When she got to the precinct and sat down at her desk, Diane looked at Jack's empty chair, opened her desk drawer, and pulled out the Menendez file. There was nothing spectacular about Samantha Menendez's murder. She had been found shot twice in the chest by a 9 mm, and witnesses saw a black man leaving the scene in a white SUV. She and Jack had spoken to Menendez's family and friends, as well as her fiancé, Carlton Watkins, and nobody could tell them who might have reason to kill the social worker from the Bronx.

"Mitchell," the lieutenant yelled from his office.

Diane got up and went to the office thinking about Kreshnik. "You wanted to see me, Lieutenant?"

"Come in and shut the door, Diane."

She did as she was asked and sat down.

"How's Jack?"

"I saw him this morning. Nothing's changed."

"Jack's a fighter, Diane. He'll make it."

"I know," she said, thinking that she would shoot the next person who told her Jack was a fighter or how strong he was. "What did you want to see me about?"

"A citizen named Besnik Duka filed a complaint with the department," the lieutenant began, and Diane swallowed hard. "He said that a woman broke into his apartment, handcuffed him, and then questioned him at gunpoint about his roommate, Lala Arapi, and his Nissan Frontier. Both just happened to have been involved in Jack's shooting."

"You want me to follow up with him?" Diane asked without hesitation.

"Really, Diane? That's what you got for me?" When the detective said nothing, the lieutenant shook his head. "Maybe if I mentioned that the woman matched your description, you'd have something to say to me."

"So you don't want me to follow up with him?"

"No, Diane, I want you to stay out of this case or get assigned a desk job. Am I making myself clear?"

"Yes, sir."

"Stand down, Diane. That's an order."

"Yes, sir," Diane said, knowing that she had already gone too far to stop now. But what was she gonna say, "I killed a man last night so here's my badge and gun"? "I'll stand down."

"Did you find out anything from him?"

"No, sir."

"Would you tell me if you did?"

"If it would catch who shot Jack, yes, sir, I would." Diane stood up. "Is that all?"

"Be careful, Diane. That's all I can say."

"Yes, sir," Diane said, and she left the precinct to reinterview Menendez's coworkers.

When that effort turned out to be just as fruitless as the last time she and Jack interviewed them, Diane went back to the hospital. Jack had not regained consciousness, so she left the hospital thinking about Samantha Menendez and rechecking her phone records, but she was driving toward the Sunset Park warehouse she had checked out earlier. As before, there was no activity at the site. Diane got back in the car and looked at the Sunny's Bar napkin and the address scribbled on it. Since she could recheck Samantha Menendez's phone records from the car, she decided to stake out the warehouse.

The detective had been there for two hours when a car parked in front of the warehouse. As she put on her gloves, Diane watched as the man got out of the vehicle and walked around to the back of the warehouse. When he disappeared into the shadows, Diane got Kreshnik's gun and got out of the car. She stayed in the shadows as she moved quietly around to the back of the building. Then she watched as the man unlocked the padlock and removed the chain. Once he unlocked and opened the door, she moved in on him quickly and put her gun to the back of his head.

"Don't move."

He raised his hands, and Diane searched him. Once she had taken his gun, the detective pushed him.

"Inside."

Once inside, her captive turned on the lights. They walked past rows of practically empty shelves until they reached a large open area. At the center of the space was a caged-off area that had three pallets of boxes on it.

"What's in there?"

"No English."

Diane hit him in the back of the head. "Open it." When the man started to unlock the cage, Diane hit him in the back of the head again. "You understand me just fine."

Her captive opened the gate and stepped in. The boxes were marked Baker's Yeast. Diane hit him in the back of the head.

"Open one!"

When he opened one of the cases, Diane motioned for him to get back. Once his back was against the fence, the detective took out her knife and cut into one of the packages. She tasted it.

"Heroin."

Thinking that she needed to call this in, Diane turned to her captive and motioned with her gun.

"Move."

With her gun returned to the back of her captive's head, she followed the man out of the cage. Diane motioned with her gun once again.

"Over there against the wall. And keep your hands up," she said when he began to lower them. Once his back was against the wall, Diane was reaching for her phone when another man came into the area.

"Who the fuck is she?" the man yelled.

When Diane turned toward him, her captive lunged at her. She shot him in the chest as the other man began shooting at her. Diane ran for cover and returned his fire. The man shot at her and ran for the door. Diane fired at him as he ran, and then she ran after him.

The detective ran out the back door and ran down the street after him. He kept firing until he had made it to his car and got in. He saw Diane coming as he started the car and drove straight at her. She stopped, raised her weapon, and kept firing at the windshield, and then she jumped out of the way as the car drove past her. The detective got to one knee and fired as she watched the car begin to slow down.

Diane approached the vehicle slowly. She could see that the man's head was on the steering wheel. One of her shots hit him in the back of the head. As she looked through the windshield, Diane saw that she had hit him once in the chest. Diane tossed Kreshnik's gun in the car.

With all that heroin inside, she still needed to call it in, and Diane went back to the warehouse. When she got inside, she found that her captive wasn't dead. He had left a trail of blood as he dragged himself across the floor. She followed the trail and caught up with him just as he reached the office. Diane shot him in the back with the gun she had taken from him and dropped it next to him.

She went into the office and called 911. Then Diane came out of the warehouse and left the scene. It was when Diane got back to the precinct that the desk sergeant called her over.

"You didn't hear this from me, but Major Case is investigating a murder that they think is connected to Jack's shooting."

"You got an address?" Diane asked and was given the address of Henricus Kreshnik. "Thanks, Sarge."

"For what?" he asked as she left the precinct.

When she arrived at the scene of her murder, Diane showed her badge and walked in. Crime scene investigators and evidence recovery technicians were processing the room. She looked on as a technician dusted for latent fingerprints on the wall where Diane had put her gun to his head and started searching him. Photographs were being taken of the spot where Kreshnik forced her to the wall and banged her hand against it until she dropped her gun and he began choking her. Another collected any physical evidence from their fight.

She could see it all as if it were happening before her eyes. She could feel his hands around her throat. She felt a twinge of pain in her back from getting thrown on the floor in the very spot she was standing.

"Mitchell," Detective Grandon shouted. "What are you doing here?" he asked when he came out of the basement.

"I heard you were here," Diane answered and walked toward him.

"You know that you're not supposed to be here."

"And I know if you're here, this has something to do with my partner getting shot."

Grandon shook his head. "Eisenberg said you were a bulldog and you weren't going to let this go."

"No, I'm not."

"Come on," Grandon said and led Diane out of the living room. "Victim's name is Henricus Kreshnik. He's a known associate of Elezi Dushku, one of the dead guys from the warehouse," he said as he led her down the stairs to the basement. As it did the last time, the smell hit her right away.

"What is that smell?" she asked as they went down the stairs.

"These guys are animals, Mitchell," he said as they got to the bottom. He pointed at the two empty cages, but Diane was looking at Kreshnik's covered body. "They were holding people in those cages. That smell is from—"

Diane held up her hand. "I get it," she said and knelt down next to the body. "What do you have on this guy?"

"He's got arrests for prostitution and arms and drug trafficking."

Diane stood up. "Any suspects?"

Grandon shook his head. "We're canvassing the neighborhood looking for witnesses and checking nearby cameras, but so far we got nothing."

"What do you think happened here?" Diane asked as they went back up the stairs.

"There was no sign of forced entry," Grandon began when they reached the ground level. "So we know that ol' Henry there let his killer in. They fought, killer forces ol' Henry downstairs. Judging from the smell, my thinking is that those cages were occupied. The killer makes Kreshnik open the cages and kills him," he said, walking Diane out of the crime scene. "Now, Detective, this was a courtesy because Eisenberg says you're a good cop, and I really do understand what you're going through. But this was a courtesy, and it won't happen again. Show me enough respect to stay out of this, and let me do my job."

"I do respect you, Detective, but I won't make you any promises," Diane said and left the scene of her murder, satisfied that for the time being she wasn't the primary suspect.

Chapter Thirty-one

Since they were interrupted the last time, when it came time for Michelle and Easy to go to school, Black told Shy that he would take them. After Shy left to go to Prestige Capital and Associates with Chuck, William brought the Alfa Romeo around and handed Black the keys. He handed them to Michelle.

"You drive."

She took the keys from her father, and he opened her door. "Thank you," she said, thinking that getting him to let her drive the Alfa when she got her keys back was going to be easier than she thought. Especially when he told her to hang on to the keys, left the car there, and rode back to the house with William.

As William drove, Black looked out the window and thought about the conversation he had after the attack at Pesce Tribeca. Once things settled down, he met in the office with Rain, Bobby, and Wanda. They listened while Monika laid out what she had planned for the Albanians. As she told Rain, her having their data gave Monika access to their entire ensemble, so she presented a number of targets for his consideration. She had already reviewed the targets she'd selected in their arms and human trafficking businesses and had moved on to the drug targets.

"Marijuana smuggled from Canada concealed in tractor-trailers, in quantities of twelve hundred pounds, stored at a warehouse in Queens," Monika offered up.

"What else?"

"I got a warehouse in Sunset Park with three hundred sixty-five kilograms of heroin hidden in thirty-three boxes marked Baker's Yeast imported from Iran." When nobody said anything, Monika continued. "There are luxury automobiles imported from Europe with kilogram quantities of cocaine concealed in hidden compartments that are stored in warehouses and stash locations throughout Brooklyn, Queens, and the Bronx," were the choices that she presented.

Black sat back and thought for a while, and then he looked at Rain. "What do you think?"

"I don't think we should do anything," Rain said, and everybody looked at her in surprise. "I don't think we need to escalate. You just reached out to Angelo. I say we wait and see if he can arrange something. If that don't work out and they come at us again, then we do the whole list in one night. That will hurt them."

Black sat without speaking, looking at Rain and thinking about what she recommended and the fact that it was she who recommended it.

"Wanda?"

"I think she's right, Mike."

"Bob?"

"I was expecting her to say kill everybody and burn the bitch to the ground, but she's right."

"Then we do nothing. For now," Black said, and Bobby took him home that night.

Therefore, since they were doing nothing, that morning after he and William had breakfast, Black went to the office. He had a meeting with Deana Butler, the head of the real estate division, that he'd been putting off all week. Now that he'd decided to do nothing, Erykah rescheduled the meeting for three that afternoon.

"Why so late?"

"It was the only time that all of them are free," Erykah said, because he would also be meeting with Jaila Bell, the head of the finance division, and Ian Jenkins, the head of the construction division.

They were meeting to discuss a fifty-four-story oceanfront glass tower project with one hundred large residences and direct-entry elevators. It would have a dramatic entrance with multiple water features, a stunning three-story lobby, an infinity pool at sea level, two sunrise and sunset swimming pools, and two hydrotherapy spas.

"There's an outdoor sky theater, and a spa with a hair and nail salon overlooking the bay," Deana said excitedly and clicked to the next slide. "There are indoor and outdoor fitness centers with a yoga and Pilates studio, a spacious indoor-outdoor dining area, and there's even an outdoor dog walk area."

As he sat there listening to his three department heads talk and sometimes yell at each other, Black heard Bobby's voice in the back of his mind.

"Every time I come to the office, you are sitting there bored out of your goddamn mind."

And he was right. Black may have been bored, but he felt that he needed to be there because this was the future that he planned for Michelle, Easy, and Mansa to inherit. Therefore, at the conclusion of Deana's presentation, he was thankful that Ian always kept his construction comments to a minimum before Jaila crunched the numbers and asked, "What do you think, Mike?"

"Let's move forward."

And that was why he was there, making decisions for his family's future.

"I'll get moving on the land acquisition right away," Deana said, and the meeting was adjourned. It was just before five when Black came into the lobby and William stood up.

"Good night, Lenecia," Black said as he passed with William.

"Have a good night, Mr. Black," she said as William blew her a kiss on his way out.

Lenecia had already transferred the phones to the night operator as security locked the front door behind William. When Reeva came into the lobby, Lenecia put on her shoes, got her purse from the drawer, and stood up.

"You ready?"

"Ready," she said, coming around the desk and heading for the door. "Good night," she said to the security guard as he unlocked the door for her and Reeva to leave.

"Where do you wanna hang out?" Lenecia asked as they drove away from Prestige Capital and Associates.

"Well, if we didn't have to be at work in the morning, and since its ladies' night, I'd say Club Obsession."

"Club Obsession? I haven't been there in years." Lenecia made a left turn and headed in that direction. "Don't look like that, Reeva. I promise that I'll have you back to your car before midnight."

When they got to Club Obsession, it was crowded, and they went to the bar to order. They stood there, waiting for the bartender and looking at all the men.

"On the house, ladies," he said, as the music exploded.

"That's my jam!" Lenecia shouted and dragged Reeva out on the dance floor, and that was when she saw Richmond.

Reeva wanted to let Lenecia know that she was going back to the bar to talk to Richmond, but when she turned to her, Lenecia was dancing with somebody. It wasn't long after that Reeva was telling Lenecia that she would see her in the morning, and she left Club Obsession with Richmond. They went to the nearest hotel.

Reeva felt the passion in his kiss. It felt as if he had real affection for her and not just a desire to be inside her. She felt herself getting wetter from his kiss as his hands roamed over her body. Richmond slowly unbuttoned her blouse. Reeva reached for his dick, stroked it through his pants, and felt it getting hard and swelling in her hand. Richmond groaned out.

"I need to get you out of these clothes."

Richmond pulled out a condom from his wallet and covered himself. Reeva knelt on the bed, and he quickly thrust himself powerfully inside her.

"Shit."

He was so thick and hard pummeling her spot. She was leaning on her elbows, working her hips into each hard thrust. He slammed into her, forcing whimpers of ecstasy to escape her lips. Reeva felt herself coming, making her walls spasm so hard that all she could do was hold on to the sheets as tight as she could, shaking and cumming.

Her body fell limp on the bed. Richmond was still hard inside of her, caressing her hips and rocking into her slowly. Reeva felt contentment as she pushed back into him gently. In that moment, she was glowing with warmth. Her entire body felt wonderful. Reeva felt completely drained and rejuvenated somehow at the same time. She curled up next to Richmond and allowed herself to drift to that place.

"I gotta go," she said.

"We can stay, and I'll take you home in the morning," he offered.

"No, I left my car at the office, and I have an early meeting," she lied because she didn't want to stay in the hotel. "You don't mind, do you?"

He kissed her. "Not at all," he said and started to get out of bed, but Reeva stopped him.

"You don't have to rush," Reeva said, and Richmond put his arm around her.

In another hotel room, in another part of the city, Lendina Neziri sat alone thinking about what he was going to do next. He was the Mik to Besnik Dervishi, the Krye of the Troka Clan, and his responsibility was to coordinate the clan's activities. But Dervishi had given him a very important job to do. Saemira Vetone, the bookkeeper for the Troka Clan, had been careless. He left sensitive data on transactions, dates, times, contacts, and locations unprotected. Elias Colton seduced Vetone's daughter, Elvana, and he had convinced her to betray her father, and she gave him the data. His job was to get it back.

Simple.

Right?

But it wasn't.

Since Colton had been avoiding him, Neziri sent Beason a video of him standing over Susan with a knife in his hand while she was asleep in their bed. After receiving the video, Beason rushed out of his office and led Neziri straight to Colton's Midtown condo.

"You know what I came for. Get it."

And that should have been that. But he let an old man, who was much stronger than he looked, trick him into the office and get the better of him. Had he known that the data was on the Surface Pro that was sitting on the coffee table and not the desktop in the office, he would have shot them both and taken the tablet, and the matter would be closed.

But it wasn't.

When Beason showed up in Switzerland without the data and claimed that he dropped it on the plane, he dispatched Ismail Flamur to search the apartment of the flight attendant they believed found it. He not only didn't find the data, but Flamur got his ass kicked by some woman. Neziri thought it was funny, saying, "You let a girl kick your ass." That was, until he sent men to kill her, and he never heard from them again.

Neziri then sent two men to kidnap the mother of the flight attendant and exchange her for the data. They reported that the flight attendant was on her way to make the exchange, and that was the last he'd heard from them. Having lost enough men to this woman, Neziri turned his attention back to Beason, but it was too late. He had unleashed Rain Robinson on the clan. Besnik Dervishi was not happy with his progress, and now his life was at stake.

Now it was time for him to tie up loose ends, and that meant that he needed to find Beason and kill him. Beason got away after the shootout with the police, but Neziri had taken his phone. He looked at the numbers that Beason had called. Thinking that those calls were Beason searching for the data or help getting it, Neziri began calling the numbers Beason dialed.

After picking up her car from the parking lot at Prestige Capital and Associates, Reeva walked in the door, kicked off her heels, and was about to get undressed when her phone rang. Thinking that it was Richmond calling to make sure that she made it home as he said he would, Reeva answered without looking at the display.

"I made it home safely," she said, and there was silence on the line. "Hello? Richmond? Hello?"

"Who is this?" Neziri asked.

When she looked at the display, she saw that it was the same number that Beason had called from, and Reeva quickly hung up the phone.

Chapter Thirty-two

A few hours later when Shy's alarm went off, the morning ritual began, and Mr. and Mrs. Black got out of bed. Once they had showered and dressed, they left their room, and Black knocked once on Michelle's door.

"Get up."

"But I don't want to!"

"You're old enough for your wants to hurt you. Get up."

"Yes, Daddy."

And then he went to wake up Easy. When he came out of Easy's room and saw Shy going downstairs with Mansa, Black knew that she wasn't going to work again that day. After breakfast, Black rode with William when he took Michelle and Easy to school, and then he came home to find his wife back in bed.

As he got undressed to join her, Black thought back to those mornings before they began playing legit businesspeople. Those days, Shy would take the children to school, and when she came home and got back in bed with him, they'd make love all morning. He got under the covers thinking about recapturing that experience and making love to Shy all morning, but then he thought about it. This was the second day in a row she didn't go to the office, and she'd left and come home early the day before that.

"You okay?" he asked, snuggling up behind her and putting his arm around her.

"I'm fine. I was just thinking about what Bobby said about us."

"Yeah, I let him get in my head about that too."

"The other day, I was sitting in my office when I realized that I had been there for almost three hours and all I had done was check my email, scroll my Facebook feed, and read an article on ending daylight saving time. I had no meetings scheduled that day, so I just came home."

He kissed her shoulder. "I know what you mean. I was there all day doing nothing, waiting for a three o'clock meeting."

"What was the meeting about?"

"I've been putting off meeting with Deana all week to discuss the oceanfront tower project."

"Were Jaila and Ian there?"

"Yes." He chuckled. "Deana likes to spend money, and Jaila is cheap, so they went round and round about the money."

"At least it was entertaining for you. My meetings consist of Reeva telling me what she's doing and me saying that it sounds good. Like I said, she runs the business. I just show up every day."

"I don't think that there is anything wrong with what we're doing. We're building a future for our children. We just need to do it in a way that doesn't make us feel so . . ."

"Phony? Is that the word you're looking for? Because that's what Bobby called me. A phony. A fake, trying to be something I'm not," she laughed. "Sitting there knowing that I would rather be out there with Rain and Monika trading shots with the Albanians than sitting in that damn meeting."

At nine o'clock sharp, Reeva parked her car in the parking lot at Prestige Capital and Associates and rushed inside, looking for but not seeing Shy's Mercedes-Maybach. She was glad that Lenecia was on a call when she came in. All she had to do was wave and keep it moving to her office. But then she thought about it and waited until Lenecia transferred the call.

"How was your night?" Lenecia asked, looking forward to hearing a juicy story about a steamy night.

"It was good. I'll tell you all about that later. Has Lavonne Reynard come in yet?"

"He's not in yet. Why, is everything all right?"

"Everything is fine. I just need to talk to him."

"I'll have him call you when he gets in," Lenecia promised, and Reeva went to her office. Once she got settled, she got to work.

It was after ten o'clock when she realized that Shy still hadn't made it in and Lavonne Reynard hadn't called her. She was about to call him when her phone rang.

"Good morning, this is Reeva."

"Ms. Duckworth, Lavonne Reynard calling. Sorry to take so long getting back to you. I was running late this morning. What can I do for you?"

"I got another call last night."

"From Beason?"

"No. It was the same number, but it wasn't Daniel. It was a man with some type of European accent."

"Have you called the police?"

"No, I wanted to talk to you or Mrs. Black first."

"What does she think?"

"She isn't in this morning."

"Okay, Ms. Duckworth. You sit tight, and I'll reach out to the police," Reynard promised. When he hung up with Reeva, he called Erykah, who promptly called Detective Mitchell.

When she got Erykah's call, Diane was at her desk, sipping coffee and staring at the Menendez file, hoping that a clue, or better yet the killer's name and address, would magically appear. She listened to what Erykah had to say and thought about going out there but thought better of it.

"Please apologize to Mrs. Black and tell her that I'm off the case and it has been reassigned to the Major Case Squad."

"Would you mind if I ask why you're off the case?"

"My partner, Detective Harmon, was shot, and they felt that I was too close to the investigation."

"I am so sorry to hear that. Is he all right?"

"He is still in intensive care," Diane said. "But I will give Detective Grandon a call and give him the information."

"Thank you, Detective Mitchell. I will let Mrs. Black know, and I'll tell Mr. Reynard to expect Detective Grandon's call. And once again, I am very sorry about your partner. I hope he'll be all right," Erykah said, and her next call was to Shy.

"I'll be right there," Shy said, and she started to get out of bed.

"What's going on?" Black asked.

"Reeva got another call from Daniel Beason, and Erykah said that Jack Harmon's been shot," Shy said on her way to the bathroom. "I'm going down there."

"Is Jack gonna be all right?"

"He's still in intensive care," Shy said and closed the bathroom door.

Once she was dressed, Shy got Chuck, and he drove her to the office. Black had just rolled over and tried to go back to sleep when his phone rang.

"Hello."

"Morning, Mike."

"Good morning, Meka. How are you doing?"

"I'm great. Are you coming to the office this morning?"

"I hadn't planned on it. Why, what's up?"

"I met with Deana and Jaila about the oceanfront tower project this morning."

"What's the problem?"

"There is some disagreement on how much leeway Deana has in negotiating the price on the land."

"You're kidding, right?"

"I am not."

"They're both sitting right in front of you, aren't they?" he chuckled.

"Yes, Mike, that is the case."

"What did you tell them?"

"I told Jaila that Deana has as much leeway as she needs to make the deal."

"And the problem is?"

"Jaila insisted that you approved the fixed amount she presented yesterday, and she insisted that I call you for clarification," Meka said, and then she was treated to the sound of Black's robust laugh.

"Tell Jaila that the amount is fixed, and tell Deana that she and I will talk about any amount above that."

"I'm sure that answer will be acceptable to both of them. Thank you, Mike."

"You're welcome. Anything else?"

"That's all I got. How are you doing?"

"I got an Albanian problem that I have to resolve, but other than that, I'm awesome."

"Albanians?" Meka questioned. "Do you want me to reach out to Oleg's people, see if maybe they can help you resolve your issue?"

"Oleg. Why didn't I think of him? Thank you, Meka. You are totally magnificent."

"You're welcome. I don't know what I did or how it helped, and I know I don't need to know, so you have a good day, Mike. I'll pass your instructions on to Deana and Jaila."

"Bye, Meka." Black ended the call, and he reached out to his old drinking buddy and business partner Oleg Mushnikov.

After spending seventeen years as a mid-level agent in the KGB's foreign intelligence wing, Oleg got involved with members of the Izmaylovskaya mob, running drug, prostitution, and gambling rings in Sri Lanka. They were introduced by Angelo, and the three used to drink together sometimes. Oleg and Black became business partners when he tried to shake Jada West down for 20 percent of her business and she turned to Black for help. Since they were looking for a partner in eastern Europe, he offered Oleg a share in a multimedia switching-gear business to leave Jada alone.

"I'm sure this will be far more lucrative for you than Ms. West's little pussy business," was what Black told Oleg the day that they became partners, and it had been a lucrative arrangement for both of them.

"This is unfortunate," Oleg said when he called Black back an hour later. "But for you, Mikhail, I will make inquiries, and I will get back to you when I have accomplished my task."

"Thank you, my friend," Black said, and he relaxed.

Later that afternoon when it came time to pick up Michelle and Easy, Black rode with William to pick them up. When he got home, Shy was back from the office.

"How's Reeva?"

"She's fine. A little shaken up, but she's fine. She's got a date tonight, and she said that she is not going to let this keep her from living her life."

"Good for her. What did the cops say?"

"Nothing much. Lavonne said that the police had been tracking the phone he called from. He overheard the detectives say that the call originated from the Valentino Pier area of Brooklyn."

"That's interesting."

"I'm sure you'll tell me why it's interesting."

"Susan said that she and Daniel met Neziri at a bar near Valentino Pier."

"That is interesting. When did you talk to Susan?" Shy asked.

Chapter Thirty-three

"Zanthia Herring, you're under arrest for the murder of Samantha Menendez."

The name and address of her killer may not have magically appeared to her, but sometimes it just pays to be lucky. Earlier in the day, as Diane sat at her desk, sipping coffee and staring at the Menendez file, Officer Kenneth Lanier walked up to her desk and said that he had somebody he was sure she'd want to talk to. Diane closed the file and stood up.

"Lead the way."

As they walked, Officer Lanier explained to the detective that he had a suspect in custody, Melissa Stinson, who was caught speeding in a white SUV.

"Since there was a BOLO for a vehicle matching that description, and Miss Stinson was acting suspicious, I searched the vehicle."

"What did you find?"

"I found a small quantity of cocaine. But as soon as I cuffed her, Stinson wouldn't stop talking about a murder she knew about."

"Wouldn't shut up, huh?" she laughed.

"I could barely finish reading her her rights." He stopped at the door. "Strap in. She's a wild ride," Lanier said as he opened the door to the interrogation room. "Miss Stinson, this is Detective Mitchell." Diane sat down. "Tell the detective what you told me."

"Okay, so a month ago, Zanthia calls and says to me, 'I need you to take me somewhere,' because her car is in the shop, so she needs me to take her somewhere. So while we're riding, she's going off and whatever about this woman and how she fucked her man behind her back and this and that, and how he done dumped her for this woman, and how she disrespected her, and she wasn't havin' none of that shit, and how she gonna settle this shit with her woman to woman—"

"Wait!" Diane held up her hand to stop her. "Slow down and take a breath." She paused, and Officer Lanier gave her an "I told you so" look. "Who is Zanthia?"

"Zanthia Herring. She's my friend who was riding with me."

"And who is the other woman?"

"Samantha Menendez. She's the one who fucked her man behind her back."

"Okay. What happened next?"

"She says she gonna get this bitch, and she tells me to pull over and park, and she says she was gonna be right back and she gets out." Stinson took a second to make sure that the next point was clear to Diane. "Now I didn't see nobody shoot nobody, but I heard the shots, and then Zanthia ran back to the car and said, 'Drive.'"

With her cold case closed, Diane was about to head out for the night and drop by the hospital to see Jack before she went home to drink, stare at the walls, and not sleep. She was on her way to her car when Diane thought about Reeva Duckworth getting a call from Daniel Beason. Knowing that Grandon wouldn't share anything with her that he'd learned from talking to Reeva, Diane decided that she would take another approach.

"Wanda Moore and Associates, this is Lavonne Reynard speaking."

"Good evening, Mr. Reynard. This is Detective Mitchell."

"Evening, Detective Mitchell. What can I do for you?"

"I was curious to know how Ms. Duckworth's interview with Detective Grandon went."

"First, let me say that I was very sorry to hear about your partner. I hope he'll be all right."

"Thank you. I appreciate that."

"Now Ms. Duckworth told the detective that she got a call from the same number as before, but it wasn't Daniel Beason calling. She said that the caller spoke with a European accent."

"Anything else?"

"There wasn't anything else, but I did hear Detective Grandon tell his partner that they had been monitoring Beason's phone and the call originated from the Valentino Pier area of Brooklyn."

"Thank you, Mr. Reynard."

"You're welcome, Detective Mitchell. Have a good night."

Diane ended the call and took out her phone and did a search on Valentino Pier, and then she dug around in her purse until she found the bar napkin that she found at the house where she killed Kreshnik.

"Sunny's Bar," Diane said and drove out to Brooklyn.

After having dinner with his family, Black had William take him to Bobby's house, and then he gave him the night off. When he arrived at the house, Wanda was there. Naturally, Bobby wanted to talk about Rain and what Black was going to do about her backing Gavin Caldwell, but Wanda wanted to talk about something else.

"I'm getting married."

"What?" Bobby asked in shock.

"James asked me to marry him, and I said yes."

Black stood up and hugged her. "Congratulations, Wanda."

"Congratulations," Bobby said, and he hugged her too.

"Seems that you guys weren't the only ones who miss me being in New York," Wanda said as Bobby went into the kitchen and got a bottle of champagne to celebrate.

Wanda had been seeing James Austin for years. At the time, she was just getting ready to begin the process of buying the bank in Nassau. So being an international lawyer was one of the first things that attracted her to him. For the first two years, she tried to keep the relationship a secret, but that wasn't happening. It wasn't a secret because Rain believed that, in her position and for security reasons, she needed to know who Wanda was involved with and put Monika on it. She worked up a complete dossier on him. So everybody was surprised when her not-so-secret man escorted Wanda to Nick's wedding. When she took her seat at the table was the first time that Wanda introduced James to her family.

With the Austin Law Firm having regional offices located in twenty states, James worked primarily out of his New York and Los Angeles offices. With both Wanda and James always being busy and also requiring their space, that was working fine for both of them. What changed things was when Wanda opened the bank and practically moved to Nassau.

Now when Wanda came to New York, it was generally on business. Therefore, she might be there for a day, maybe two. They'd get together, have dinner, make love, and she'd be back on Jada's jet in the morning. It wasn't much different when she'd visit him in Los Angeles: dinner, sex, and jet. And when James would come to Nassau to see Wanda, the only thing that was different was that he would stay three or four days, and then he had to go. James missed Wanda, and he wanted the cycle to stop.

"So when's the big day?" Bobby asked as he popped the cork and poured the champagne.

"We haven't set a date yet."

"Then you're not pregnant, and this won't be a shotgun wedding," Bobby joked.

"No, Bobby, I'm not pregnant, and I want this to be a big, 'pull out all the stops,' over-the-top, extreme wedding." *Definitely bigger than Nick and April's wedding.* "And I want both of you to give me away."

"I would be honored," Bobby said.

"So would I, Wanda," Black said. "And I am going to throw you the biggest wedding fit for the queen you are."

"What's all the commotion about?" Pam asked when she came into the room.

"I'm getting married," Wanda exclaimed and hugged Pam.

"Congratulations, Wanda," Pam said. "I hope that you and James will be very happy." She paused. "You are marrying James, right?"

Wanda laughed. "Yes, Pam, I am marrying James."

Bobby handed Pam a glass, and they all raised their glasses. "To long life and happiness."

"To a long-lasting and happy marriage," Pam said.

"To you, my friend," Black said, and they drank to the bride-to-be.

It was Bobby who brought an end to the celebratory mood when he asked what Black planned to do about Rain.

"I decided to take your advice."

Bobby shook his head. "One of them damn tests."

Wanda laughed. "What's the latest with the Albanians?"

"I reached out to Oleg to see if he can't put us in touch with somebody with power in the clan." He looked at Bobby. "You remember Susan said that she met Neziri at Sunny's Bar near Valentino Pier?"

"Yeah."

"Cops said that Beason's phone was used last night, and the call originated from the Valentino Pier area."

"Interesting," Bobby said.

"Who's Susan?" Wanda asked.

"His new Jada," Bobby said and laughed.

"No, Mike." Wanda frowned.

"She is not my new Jada," Black said, frowning and shaking his head. "Susan is married to the guy suspected of killing Quentin and Elias Colton."

"And she's Mike's type," Bobby said, still laughing. "And she doesn't try hard to keep it a secret that she wants to fuck him."

"That makes it dangerous," Wanda giggled. "For her. Shy will kill her."

"She already threatened to put a bullet in her brain," Bobby said, laughing, and then he saw that Black wasn't having as much fun with it as he and Wanda were. "Let me stop fuckin' with you."

"Thank you."

Although Black adored his wife and had no intention of cheating on her, he had to admit that Susan was fine as hell, and Bobby was right. She was his type. When he started seeing women again after he was led to believe that his wife was murdered, he gravitated to Mystique. Her name was Maria Harrow, and she looked and was built so much like Shy that Bobby called her Amazon Shy. Then he started seeing CeeCee. Her statuesque beauty rivaled Mystique's, and then CeeCee began making herself useful to him. And then came Jada West. He wanted her the first time he saw her. In those days, she used to dance at a club called Ecstasy, and she went by the name Miss Kitty.

If he wanted to be completely honest with himself, he would have to admit that Susan was just seductive enough to make him want her, so it was best that he stay away from her.

"So you wanna ride out to Brooklyn and check out that bar?" Bobby asked.

Glad that Bobby had dropped it, Black stood up. "Let's go." He looked at Wanda. "You wanna ride, soldier?"

"Not tonight. I have a late date with James."

Black hugged Wanda. "I am so happy for you."

"Thank you, Mike."

Bobby hugged her too, and then they left Bobby's house and headed out to Brooklyn to check out Sunny's, a little bar near Valentino Pier in Brooklyn.

Diane parked her car on Conover Street and looked at the old green truck that was parked out front and went inside. The detective looked around the cozy little place whose walls were covered with local art. There was a nice crowd, and the live music playing made for a fun atmosphere. She was about to go to the bar to get a drink when Diane saw Neziri and another man leaving through the back door.

"This is it," Bobby said, looking at the old green truck as they went inside Sunny's.

"There's Detective Mitchell," Black said, pointing as she followed Neziri out the back door.

When she got outside, Diane stood in the shadows and saw Neziri and the man with him walk down the alley to another building, and they went inside. Once they were out of sight, the detective followed them to the building.

Black and Bobby came out the back door of Sunny's in time to see Diane go into the building.

"Fuck is she going?" Bobby asked as they followed her down the alley.

Once inside the building, Diane heard talking coming from the second floor. She took out her weapon

and moved slowly up the stairs. As she moved far-
ther up the stairs, the voices got louder. The detective
reached the top of the stairs, and there were two doors.
She approached quietly and then listened. With her
weapon drawn, she kicked in the door.

"Lendina Neziri! You're under arrest for the attempted
murder of Detective Jack Harmon!" she shouted and
immediately took cover as Neziri, the man with him,
and three other men in the room all opened fire.

Outside the building, Black and Bobby heard the
shooting. They ran into the building and followed
the sound of gunfire until they entered the room where
Diane was taking heavy gunfire from five shooters.

As Neziri and his men sprayed the room with bullets
from automatic weapons, Black and Bobby opened fire,
and that gave the detective a chance to get to better cover.
Black raised his weapon and shot one in the head. Black
and Bobby kept firing. When Diane made it to cover, she
began firing.

When one stopped to reload a fresh clip, Bobby stood
up and hit him with two shots to the chest. The man
went down. Diane emptied her clip and then dropped to
reload. She saw Neziri. He continued firing as he moved
to take cover behind a desk. Diane stayed low to the floor
until she had a clear shot at him, but she had to take
cover as one of his men began firing at her.

Neziri stood up, fired a few shots, and made a run for it.

"I got him!" Diane yelled and went after him.

When Diane ran out the door, Black and Bobby moved
in on the two remaining shooters. They opened fire and
kept firing until one's weapon was empty, and he took
cover to reload. He was about to load it when Black shot
him in the head. Bobby raised his weapon and fired three
shots at the last shooter. Each shot hit him in the chest,
and he went down. Bobby stood over him and put two in
his head as Black ran after Diane.

The detective ran down the stairs and out of the building. She chased Neziri down the alley and back inside Sunny's. "Police!" she yelled as she entered.

Neziri turned quickly and fired at her. Some customers at Sunny's Bar hit the floor while others took cover under the tables. When he fired again and turned to leave, Neziri stumbled, and before he could get to his feet, Diane was on top of him.

"Get up!" she shouted and put her gun to Neziri's head as Black ran into Sunny's.

Diane hit him in the face with her gun.

"Detective," he shouted.

"What?" Diane shouted, hit him again, and then she shoved her gun in Neziri's mouth.

He came and stood next to her. "Remember which one of us is a cop and which one of us is a killer."

She had already killed three men. "Maybe we're more alike than I thought."

After a few tense seconds, Diane eased the gun out of his mouth slowly.

"Lendina Neziri! You're under arrest for the attempted murder of Detective Jack Harmon."

She spun him around, pushed him against the wall, and cuffed him.

"You have the right to remain silent. Anything you say can and will be used against you in a court of law. . . ."

Chapter Thirty-four

"You two should go," Diane said to Black and Bobby after she called for backup.

"You sure?"

"I'm sure." She looked at Neziri. "If he gives me any trouble, I'm sure that some of these fine citizens will be more than happy to help."

"You damn right, Officer," one citizen said.

"We're with you all the way," another said.

"We're gone," Bobby said, and he left Sunny's Bar with Black. "So," he said as they walked back to Bobby's car, "who was that?"

"I have no idea, and I didn't think the detective had time for questions. But I'm guessing, and this is based on the gun she shoved in the guy's mouth, that was the guy who shot Jack."

"So you don't know if that was the guy who killed Quentin?"

"I do not."

"So we rode all the way out here to save her life," Bobby said and unlocked the car.

"Pretty much," Black said, and he got in the car.

"Okay. We done for the night?"

"You got something to do?"

"Nope. What about you?"

"I got nowhere to go," Black said and took out his phone.

"This Rain."

"Where are you?"

"Safehouse."

"We're on our way."

"Where is she?" Bobby asked.

"Wanda's safe house."

"Wanda's got a safe house?"

"For years. Where you been?"

"Not knowing she had a safe house apparently. Where is it?"

Black told him how to get there, and Bobby headed for the Brooklyn Bridge. They were heading north on the FDR Drive when Black's phone rang.

"Who is this?" Black asked, not recognizing the number.

"Mikhail, it is your very good friend Oleg."

"Yes, my friend. How are you?"

"I am good, as always, and I have news."

"Talk to me."

"These Albanians you seek, the Troka Clan. I have arranged a meeting between you, Mikhail, and Besnik Dervishi. He is the Krye of the Troka Clan."

"Krye. That means he's the boss, right?"

"Yes, Mikhail, he is boss."

"You know this guy?"

"Only by reputation. Dervishi is a violent man, an animal, but you, Mikhail, have earned his respect. I have delivered your message, and they have agreed to meet. You return their property, and everybody walks away."

"Tell me where and when."

"Tonight. Medical building on Astor Avenue in two hours."

"Two hours?" Black paused as Bobby approached the Robert F. Kennedy Bridge. "We'll be there."

"You come with two of your men, and I will see you there," Oleg said.

"Thank you, my friend. See you in two hours." Black ended the call with Oleg, and then he called Rain. "You need to go by the office and pick up the data," he told Bobby, and he got off the FDR.

"This Rain."

"Change of plan."

"What's up?"

"Oleg arranged a meeting with the Krye of the Troka Clan."

"When and where?"

"In two hours. At a medical building on Astor Avenue."

"Two hours?"

"You heard me. The sooner we get them back their shit, the better."

"For real."

"I need you and Monika to meet me and Bobby there. Call Carla and tell her we're coming, and have the data ready. And if it's at all possible, I need her to have eyes and ears in that place. I don't wanna walk up in no trap."

"No shit. See you in two," Rain said, and she ended the call.

"What's up?" Monika asked.

"Black arranged a meeting with the Albanians in two hours at a medical building on Astor Avenue."

"Two hours?" Monika asked.

"That's what the man said, and he wants you to have eyes and ears in that place." Rain smiled. "If it's at all possible."

"I know he doesn't wanna walk up in no trap, but damn, two hours." She shook her head and picked up her phone.

"This is Carla."

"Omega, this is Alpha. I have a code black at a medical building on Astor Avenue."

"Acknowledged, Alpha. What's our window?"

"Two hours."

"Two hours?" Carla questioned as she accessed the Astor Avenue property. "Acknowledged, Alpha. Activating necessary assets."

"Do the best you can. BOTF is on his way to pick up the data."

"Acknowledged, Alpha." Carla ended the call. "Hey, Carla, pull a pink and purple polka-dot rabbit out of your ass, and do it in two hours," she said aloud and began accessing the satellites and cameras she'd need to accomplish her task.

By the time Black and Bobby arrived at the office to pick up the data, Carla was just about ready to head to the medical building on Astor Avenue. Once she had handed him the drive, Carla informed him that Xavier was at the site with the team who had protected Aunt Priscilla at the hospital. She was also able to access the building security systems.

"They do have cameras, but they only cover the hallways and access points. Once you go into a room, I am totally blind."

"Understood," Black said as he walked alongside her.

"Xavier's team is surveilling the area as we speak. Right now it's quiet around the building, but like I said, if they've already got people in those rooms . . ."

"Understood." Black stopped on his way to the door and turned to Carla. "Thank you, Carla. I know we ask you to do all kinds of shit, and you do everything we ask of you like it's just another Tuesday afternoon and it's no big deal. I just wanted you to know that I see you and I appreciate you."

"Bonus envelope!" Bobby shouted on the way out the door.

"Thank you, Mike. That means a lot to me."

"See you at the drop," he said, and they left the office and headed uptown to the medical building on Astor Avenue.

When Rain and Monika arrived in the area, she made contact with Xavier. She told him that Black and Bobby had picked up the data, they were on their way, and Carla was right behind them. He reported that the immediate area around the medical building appeared to be clear. He had operatives surveilling the front and rear of the building. "From a safe distance, of course."

"Of course," Monika said.

"If this is an ambush, it was already set," Xavier reported.

"Everybody stay out of sight and be ready."

Rain walked back to where the car was parked. She was about to get back in when she saw a man coming toward her. The closer he got, the more familiar he looked until Rain knew exactly where she knew him from. He was Ismail Flamur, the man she fought in Sapphire's apartment.

She was about to take out her gun when he recognized her. Flamur quickly pulled his gun and shot at Rain. She dove behind a car for cover as he ran. Rain got to her feet with a gun in each hand and looked around. When she saw Flamur running, she went after him. He turned and shot at her. Rain took cover and fired back. Flamur took off running, and Rain fell in behind him.

Rain ran as fast as she could and began firing at Flamur with both guns. He ducked behind some cars and fired back at her. He stayed low and kept firing shots at her until he reached the corner. He rose up, stopped, fired a couple of shots at Rain, and then took off running.

She ran after Flamur, busting shots all the way. When he wheeled around and fired at her, Rain was able to make it to cover. She shot back, but he was gone again.

"Fuck!" she shouted, reloaded her weapon, and went after Flamur again.

Rain was fast, so she was able to catch up with Flamur. He kept firing shots as he ran into an apartment building. When she got inside, Rain saw him run into a stairwell, and she went after him. She looked up at the top of the stairs and saw Flamur standing there. He fired at her, opened the door, and ran in. Rain ran up the steps. When she got to the landing, she opened the door slowly and stepped inside cautiously. She didn't see Flamur anywhere and continued down the hall.

Suddenly, a door behind her burst open. Flamur jumped out and fired a few shots at her, and then he ran back down the stairs. She went after him, leaping down the stairs to catch up. When he stopped and fired again, Rain fired back and put one in his head. She ran down the steps and shot Flamur one more time to make sure he was dead.

Chapter Thirty-five

After leaving Carla at the office, Black and Bobby headed for the meeting at the medical building on Astor Avenue. As they drove, Black was apprehensive about how this was going to go. Maybe he was overreacting, but there was nothing in their experience with the Albanians that suggested that this would go smoothly. He thought about calling Oleg and telling him to insist that the meeting had to take place at a neutral location, but it was too late for that now. One thing he was sure of—if things went south and this was an ambush, their ambushers would not get far before they met the same fate.

It caused him to think about his family. From the first day that he saw and fell desperately in love with Shy, his mission in life had been to protect her from harm. Black had moved her out of New York to the islands to accomplish it. Over the years, neither had made it easy to keep her safe. Between The Family's enemies trying to kill him and her need to be in the center of the action, they had lived in a constant state of danger.

And then they had children.

That only amplified his need to protect them. So they were trying to step back. Even though he still ran things, Black made Rain boss of The Family, and Shy hung up her guns. He smiled as he thought back to what Michelle said to Shy when she was under investigation for the murder of Andrade Ferreira and she told her daughter everything was all right.

"Then why does Daddy look like that?" Michelle pointed to her father.

"That's how he always looks when you're in trouble, and the next thing you know, we're on the Cessna heading for Freeport."

It was less than a week later that Michelle was proven right when her parents sent the family to Freeport before men blew up their house.

It made him think about something that Sonny Edwards, his old consigliere, said to him when Rain and Wanda took The Family to war over Nick.

"I know that this is who you are. The shit is in your blood, and retirement is the last thing on your mind."

Black had been denying that for years. That may have been who he was, but he was a changed man. But the changes were superficial. He may dress better these days, and he might show up at the offices of Prestige Capital and Associates to attend boring meetings, but at his core, he was still the same Mike Black in the story that he'd told his son.

"You just a vicious muthafucka, a vicious black-wearing muthafucka," and the name stuck because it was the truth. He was Vicious Black, but as Easy said, now it was only when he needed to be. That thought made him smile as Bobby parked behind Rain's car. She had parked three blocks from the medical center. They got out.

"Where's Rain?" Black asked when Monika got out of Rain's car.

"I don't know. She was here one second, and the next thing I knew, she was gone. I tried calling her, but she didn't answer. I got Xavier's team looking for her," Monika reported.

"You talk to Carla?"

"She's two minutes out."

Black looked at his watch. "Okay, they should be there soon. We need to go," he said as Rain came walking up.

"Where you been?" Monika asked.

"I saw the muthafucka who broke into Sapphire's apartment."

"Did you kill him?" Bobby asked, and Monika laughed.

"You know she did," Monika said, and Black smiled.

"You do know that we're here to sit down and make peace with these muthafuckas, right?" Bobby asked.

"And we still can. One more dead soldier ain't gonna make no difference," Rain said, and Black shook his head as he walked back to Bobby's car. She was Rain Robinson, and just as he would always be Vicious Black, she would always be the murdering so-called psychopath she was when he handed her power.

"Let's go get this over with," Black said.

"Alpha to Omega, what is your status?"

"In position and standing by." She had parked the van a block from the medical center.

Rain got into the car with Black and Bobby while Monika drove Rain's car around to join Carla in the van. When Black, Bobby, and Rain pulled up in front of the center, there were two men standing outside.

"What are we looking at, Carla?"

"Halls are clear. Four heat signatures inside."

"Thank you, Carla," Black said and ended the call. "Let's go."

Inside the center, Oleg Mushnikov waited with Besnik Dervishi, the Krye or boss of the Troka Clan. Dervishi migrated to America due to the war in Kosovo. In the years that followed, Dervishi took over the clan's heroin and prostitution networks. His Kryetar, Lule Vata, would be considered underboss of the clan, and the new Mik, or friend to the Kryetar, Prifti Shehu, was there with him. The previous Mik, Lendina Neziri, had failed in his task and would face the consequences of that failure.

When Black entered with Bobby and Rain, they were escorted to what used to be a conference room, where Oleg made the introductions. Black and Dervishi shook hands. Both men nodded, but neither said a word. Then Black shook hands with Lule Vata.

"I had a feeling that you and I would see each other again," Vata said. He and Black met the night that he, Bobby, and Wanda went to Tirana Gentlemen's Club.

"Perhaps we should have talked that night," Black said.

"Perhaps." Vata nodded. "But I was not in a talking mood that night, so perhaps things went as they should have."

"Perhaps," Black said and sat down.

As the arbiter of the sit-down, Oleg sat at the head of the table. Rain sat at the center, flanked on either side by Black and Bobby, with the Albanians on the opposite side of the table.

"Mikhail, did you bring the data?" Oleg asked once everyone was seated.

Rain removed the drive from her pocket and put it on the table in front of her. Vata, who was sitting directly across from Rain, held out his hand.

"I know that we're here for me to hand you back this shit and everybody walks away happy. But before that happens, I'm gonna say what the fuck I gotta say, and if you muthafuckas got a problem with that, then fuck you." She paused. "This is not the first time I tried to give you fucks back this shit. I tried once before, and you shot my fuckin' aunt! My fuckin' aunt! She didn't have a fuckin' thing to do with this shit, but you fucks shot her!" Rain paused. "Now we're sitting here all honorable and shit. Where was the fuckin' honor in shooting an innocent, unarmed woman? Tell me that shit!"

"Apologies for your aunt," Vata said and held out his hand.

"Apologies? And just hand you the drive." Rain shook her head. "Before that happens, you dishonorable mutha-fuckas murdered an innocent man, Quentin Hunter. Give me the name of the man who murdered him, and I'll hand over the data."

Vata glanced at Dervishi, and he nodded his head.

"Saemira Vetone."

Rain slid the drive to Vata.

"Where do I find him?" Black asked.

Saemira Vetone had been the bookkeeper for the Troka Clan for more than twenty years. He was married to Rozafa, the daughter of Erion Grezda, the former Krye of the Troka Clan. When he found out that his daughter Elvana had betrayed him, he was furious. She had shared her bed with a black man and brought shame and dishonor to his family. Her honor had to be restored by killing Elias Colton, the man who seduced his baby girl and convinced her to betray him.

Although he had never met Colton, Vetone went look-ing for him. He didn't know that Neziri had already killed him. He had met his partner, Daniel Beason, many times, and his plan was simple: force Beason to tell him where Colton was so he could kill him. However, when he ar-rived at Beason's house, Quentin Hunter was there, and, thinking that he was Colton, Vetone shot and murdered Quentin.

Nothing in the world travels faster than bad news. Therefore, it didn't take very long for Saemira Vetone to find out that he was the price of peace between the Troka Clan and The Family. Loyalty to the clan being what it was, he found himself alone. Elvana was gone, Rozafa had returned to her family, and other clan members would not take his call. The only ones willing to stand with him were two of his brothers. Vetone's other two brothers, feeling the shame and dishonor that Elvana had brought upon their family, stood with the clan.

He had booked a flight to Skopje, the capital of North Macedonia. But his Air Canada flight from LaGuardia didn't depart until ten thirty the following morning. All he had to do was survive the night and make it to the airport.

Simple, right?

But you know that it wasn't.

It was after midnight when two vehicles parked outside the home of Saemira Vetone. Black and Bobby got out of the car and got into the van with Carla and Monika. Carla had already hacked into and disabled Vetone's security system and had control of all the cameras in the house.

"What are we looking at?" Black asked and sat down.

"There are three identified targets in the house. Vetone is upstairs in the last room on the right. The other two are downstairs on the couch. None of them have moved in a while, so I think they're asleep."

"Okay." Black stood up. Bobby and Monika did too. "Where are you two going?"

"With you," Bobby said, and Monika nodded.

"Why? There's only three of them." Black put silencers on his guns. "And they're asleep." He looked at Carla. "We got this, right, Carla?"

"Right."

Bobby sat down. "Handle your business, Vicious Black."

Monika shook her head and got her guns. "All the same, I'm coming with you."

"Suit yourself. Let's go."

"It'll be like old times," Monika said and followed him out of the van.

Black and Monika went around to the back of the house. Carla had recommended that they enter the house through an open window on the south side.

"Unless you just wanna kick in the door the way we used to and go in guns blazing," Monika asked as they got to the window.

"This will do," Black said, and Monika handed him a pair of night-vision goggles. He motioned toward the window. "After you."

"Always the gentleman," Monika said and went in, and then Black followed her. They left the room and moved out into the hall and positioned themselves on the perimeter of the living room.

"Since you're here, you can play with these two. I'm going upstairs."

"Have fun." Monika waited until he had reached the stairs. "Now, Omega," she said, and Carla killed the lights. Black headed up the stairs.

"You've got movement in the living room. One target advancing on your position."

Monika raised her weapon.

"In firing range in three, two, one," Carla said, and Monika fired one shot. It hit him in the side of his head.

When his brother heard the thud of the body hitting the floor, it startled him, and he began firing wildly in that direction. The noise woke Vetone. He grabbed his gun and tried to turn on the lights.

Monika stayed out of range until she heard the clicking of an empty gun, and she watched as her prey backed against the wall. Then she walked up to him, raised her gun to his head, and pulled the trigger. When his body hit the floor, Monika headed upstairs.

Vetone sat up in the bed with his gun pointed at the door. He was a numbers guy, not a shooter, so his hands were shaking. When the door swung open, Vetone pulled the trigger and kept firing until his gun was empty. That was when Black walked into the room and sat down on the bed.

"Who are you?"

"My name is Mike Black. You killed an innocent man, and I'm here to kill you," he said, raised his weapon, and shot Vetone in the forehead. Then Black stood up and put two in his chest as Monika appeared at the door.

"See? Just like old times," she said as Black came out of the room, and they headed for the stairs.

"It was. Now let's get outta here, big ass."

"Just like old times," Monika said because he hadn't called her big ass since Shy came back from the dead.

Chapter Thirty-six

Peaches sat in the back seat, looking out the window and enjoying the scenery as her son drove her to a baby shower. Venus, RJ's ex-wife, was pregnant, and Pam was having a shower for her. Since welcoming a new member of The Family was, by definition, a family event, Shy insisted that she host the party because her house was bigger. Venus was having a boy, and that day her family and friends had gathered to pay tribute to the new man-child.

"He lives here?" Peaches asked as they turned into the driveway at Black and Shy's house.

"Yes, Ma," Baby Chris told his mother.

"Their last house got blown up," Payton said enthusiastically. The whole "I'm in love with a gangster" thing still excited her.

Peaches shook her head. "He's come a long way from that tiny apartment he used to live in."

Baby Chris looked in the rearview at his mother and got out of the car wondering how well she knew the boss of The Family. The reason he invited her was that Black always asked about her.

"Tell Peaches don't be a stranger. She's family."

Inside the house, the soon-to-be grandparents, Bobby and Pam, as well as Venus's parents were celebrating with the parents-to-be. It was a chance for the grandparents to spend some time getting to know each other before their future grandchild arrived. Since Venus now lived at the house with the Rays, Pam was deeply involved with getting everything prepared for the new bundle of joy.

As had become customary at family events, Chuck was controlling access to the media room, where Black was talking to family members about their issues and concerns, settling disputes, and granting wishes. As host of the party, Shy was wandering around her house, seeing to it that everybody was having a good time.

"Hello, Mrs. Black."

"Hey, BC, how are you doing?"

"I'm fine, Mrs. Black. I want to introduce you to my mother, Peaches."

"Peaches." Shy smiled. "Finally. I have heard so much about you from so many people."

"Likewise. The famous Shy, the woman who won't die," Peaches said and laughed.

Easy heard her say that and he immediately went off in search of Michelle for an explanation.

"It's nice to meet you, Peaches."

She turned to Payton. "And this is Payton Cummings."

"One day you have to tell me what it's like to jump out of an airplane. I always think about doing stuff like that, but I am just too chicken to actually do it."

Payton had famously jumped out of an airplane to commit a minor robbery along with three of her friends just for the thrill of it. That didn't turn out well for her friends, because some risks aren't worth taking and some thrills you can do without.

"I would be happy to go up with you anytime you wanna try it," Payton said.

"I just may take you up on that," Shy said and moved on to speak with other guests.

Wanda had come to the shower with her new fiancé, James Austin. However, since this was Venus's day, she decided to save her announcement for another day.

They were sitting in the Blacks' living room along with the soon-to-be grandparents as Venus received gifts. Although RJ and Venus weren't together, he was totally committed to being a father to his son, so he was sitting next to her.

But then there were members of The Family who did not come bearing gifts. Those members of The Family handed Venus cash-filled envelopes, which she happily placed in a silk floral print bag that Wanda gave her for the occasion, which matched the outfit she was wearing. By the end of the evening, that little silk bag would have close to $100,000 in it.

Chuck stuck his head in the door to the media room. "I got Ryder out here to see you."

"Send her in."

"You got her," Chuck said and swung the door open for Ryder to come in.

Black stood up to greet his wife's oldest and closest friend. Her real name was Dale, but growing up, she got teased because Dale was a boy's name. That ended when she got fed up and started kicking ass.

"Thank you for seeing me, Mike."

"Have a seat, and tell me, what can I do for you?"

"It's not what you can do. I mean, I don't want nothing. I just need some advice."

"On what?"

"It's just that I don't feel like I get the respect I think I deserve."

"Why is that? Everybody I know—and I know everybody in this family—everybody I know respects you and the work you do. I know that I do."

"Thank you, Mike, but it's like"—she paused and leaned forward—"when something is going on in The Family and there's a captains' meeting, I never hear about it."

"You've been captaining Carter's crew for years, and you were Jab's brain before that. That sounds like a captain to me. You should be there."

"What should I do?"

"Do you remember what I told you after that business with Jab?"

"You said that I needed to surround myself with people who would be loyal to me."

"Did you do that?"

"Yes."

"I know. That's your crew. Sounds like a captain to me. You build on that."

"Is that 'Mike Black: businessman' talking, or 'Mike Black: boss of this family'?"

"Aren't they the same person?"

"I guess they are."

"You never have to worry about your position in this family. My advice is to keep doing what you're doing. The people who matter see you and respect your work. And you let me worry about your title," he said, knowing that now that they were done dealing with the Albanians, he was going to have that talk with Rain. He would address it with her then. "Tell me, what's going on with you and Truck?"

"Nothing I can't handle."

Black stood up. "You let me know when you can't."

Ryder stood up. "That will never happen."

By the time Alwan arrived at the house, the driveway was full of cars, so he parked on the street. Rain got out and waited while Alwan got the Priam stroller she had gotten for the baby shower, and then they walked to the house. As she made her way to the living room to pay tribute and deliver her gift, Rain bumped into Shy.

During the days when Rain was working with Black, she was damn near living at their old house. She had a room of her own and definitely ate there every day. Since both she and Shy loved to eat and neither could cook, and they were both addicted to M's cooking, a bond was formed. They hadn't seen each other since Michelle's party.

"What's up, Shy?"

"Hey, girl."

Shy hugged her, and then she stepped back and looked at Rain.

"What?"

Shy's eyes narrowed as she leaned close to Rain. "Are you pregnant?" she whispered.

Rain's eyes opened wide. She grabbed Shy's hand and led her out of the house. "How do you know?" she asked the second she closed the door.

"You look pregnant. Belly a little rounded, breasts a little fuller, and you're glowing," Shy said softly as Reeva began coming up the stairs carrying a gift for the baby. "Hi, Reeva. I'm so glad that you could make it."

"Thank you for inviting me."

"Reeva, this is my friend Rain Robinson."

"Nice to meet you, Rain," Reeva said, a little intimidated because she'd heard the office gossip about Rain Robinson.

Shy opened the door for her guest. "Come on inside, and I'll introduce you to the soon-to-be mother and father." She leaned close to Rain. "We'll talk later," Shy said and followed Reeva inside.

When Rain went back into the house, Alwan was still standing in the spot where she left him with the big box in his hands. "Let's get this over with and get outta here."

She headed for the living room to deliver her gift, but it took a while for her to get there because, as she made her way through the crowd of family members, some shared their issues and concerns with her. Once she delivered her gift to the parents-to-be, Pam introduced Rain to Venus's parents. Since she knew, she discreetly congratulated Wanda and James on their engagement and was on her way to the door when she ran into Michelle.

"Hi, Aunt Rain." Michelle hugged her. "Daddy wants to see you before you go."

"Okay. Where is he."

"In the media room," Michelle said and led Rain to the media room, where Chuck was still controlling access.

"What's up, Chuck? Somebody in there with him?"

"Money's in there," he said.

So Rain had to wait, but it wasn't long before the door opened, and Black walked out with Marvin.

"Thank you, Uncle Mike."

"No problem. I'll tell Frank to stop being such a dick about everything," Black said to Marvin, and that was when he noticed that Savannah Russell had come there with him. She was Frank Sparrow's assistant and his former lover.

Now I understand why Frank's being a dick about everything.

Frank had gotten Marvin's fighter, Alex "The Bronx Bomber" Benton, on the undercard of the middleweight championship fight between Genesis Rodriguez and Jacques Gauthier, and now Frank was trying to renegotiate Marvin's share of the pay-per-view money.

Black looked at Rain. "Come on in."

When Black and Rain went into the room, Chuck closed the door, and Michelle walked away, thinking back to the days when she would be in that room with her father.

"What's up?"

Black sat down. "Tell me what you haven't told me about you and Gavin Caldwell."

Rain sat down and told her story.

"Why didn't you tell me?"

"Honestly?"

"Is there another way?"

"I knew I shouldn't have done it."

"That was all the more reason for you to tell me."

"You're right. How'd you find out?" she asked because it was important.

"Your captains didn't betray you if that's what you're asking."

"It is."

"Angelo told me about the task force having a witness to Gavin and a woman in a blond wig and sunglasses killing Greg Mac."

"Oh." Rain held up her hand. "I know. I need a better disguise than a blond wig and sunglasses."

"Thank you for not making me say it." He smiled. "I was impressed when Angee said he was murdered while in police custody, but do you think you showed the best judgment when you decided to involve us in Gavin's business?"

"No."

"And that's why you didn't tell me." Black paused and Rain nodded. "I have to be honest with you, it made me question the trust that I have in you. I thought that I needed to test your judgment, but the last few days showed me that I neither need to test nor question your judgment. At every turn, you showed good judgment. Even when I was ready to go hard at them, you were the one showing restraint. That's good judgment."

"So what happens now?"

"Even though it was suggested, I'm not going to exile you to an island in the Caribbean."

"Wanda?"

"Yes, but then she pointed out that even though you backed Gavin's play, you did avoid getting us in the middle of his war with Kojo, and you kept us off the task force's radar. So what happens now is this can never happen again between you and me."

"Understood," she said and left the office.

Rain was on her way to the door with Alwan when she ran into Shy again.

"Don't leave. We need to talk."

Damn, she thought and went back into the living room, passing Barbara on the way.

"Hey, Aunt Rain," Barbara said.

"What's up?"

Barbara had come to the celebration with her some-time boyfriend, Cole Montgomery. Rain looked him up and down.

"You still around?" Rain asked.

"Yes, ma'am," he said, somewhat frightened, as he remembered Rain threatening to hunt him down and shoot his dick off.

Rain shook her head and kept it moving. Barbara may have come to the party with Cole, but her eyes were on Marvin. He was getting in the buffet line with Savannah.

He really is kinda fine, she thought.

Her girlfriend, LaSean, who was helping Barbara set up her online gambling operation, had been going on and on about how fine her cousin Marvin was and how she wouldn't mind getting with him since the day Barbara introduced them.

But Marvin wasn't her cousin.

"Come on, Cole. I'm hungry," she said and headed for the buffet line.

Marvin saw her coming, and he thought back to all the times that Sataria used to try to convince him that he was cheating on her with Barbara. Each time he would tell her how ridiculous it was because Barbara was his cousin.

But Barbara wasn't his cousin.

And Barbara is fine as hell, he thought as she got in line behind them.

"Hey, Barbara. You look nice today."

"You're not looking too bad yourself." She smiled. "You remember my friend Cole?"

"What's up, man?" Marvin said. He shook his hand and turned to Savannah. "Barbara, this is my friend Savannah Russell. My cousin, Barbara."

"Nice to meet you, Barbara," Savannah said politely.

"We met at the fight party at my club," Barbara reminded her.

"We certainly did," Savannah said as she got a plate and began getting her food.

It was just about that time that Shy was walking to the door with Reeva, thanking her for coming. "Thank you again for inviting me. I had a nice time, but I promised some people that I'd meet them at Surface."

"Another date with Richmond?"

"No, just meeting some friends."

"Well, you have a good time, and I'll see you Monday," Shy said as Reeva went down the stairs, and she went back into the house. Rain was standing by the door. "Come on," Shy said, grabbing Rain by the hand and dragging her into the media room.

"Before you say anything, yes, I am pregnant."

"Does Michael know?"

"I haven't told him. But knowing Black, he knows."

"You gonna have it?"

"No, I'm not."

"If you need somebody to go with you, I'm here for you."

"Thank you, Shy. I was going to get it done on Monday." Thinking Shy would be more supportive than Alwan, she added, "And I would love for you to come with me."

"Come with you where?" Black asked when he came into the media room.

"Shopping," Shy said quickly.

"Yeah, I hate to shop," Rain said.

Black sat down. "You in a hurry?"

"Not really. What's up?" Rain sat down. Shy sat next to Black.

"You think we're done with the Albanians?"

"I hope so."

"The police never did find Daniel, did they?" Shy asked.

"No. Detective Mitchell arrested the guy who shot Jack. Maybe he can tell her where he is."

"You know what I can't figure out?" Shy said.

"What's that, Cassandra?"

"How Reeva Duckworth fits into the story."

Chapter Thirty-seven

After leaving the baby shower, Reeva was on her way to Surface, an elite cocktail lounge, to meet her coworkers: Sharonda Noel, the assistant VP of artist development; Cheryl Valle, who was Gladys Gordon's assistant; and Lenecia, of course.

They had been there for over an hour, and everybody was having a good time when Reeva saw Richmond come in. She immediately got excited as thoughts of the love they made filled her mind. Reeva was imagining Richmond kissing her while he pumped hard in and out of her. Just the thought of it had her womb clenching hard when she saw that he wasn't there alone. Richmond was with the woman with the purple braids, whom she had seen him with at the Lit Lounge.

Reeva sat angrily with her heart pounding as she watched Richmond go to the bar. As he waited for the bartender, he stood behind purple braids, wrapped his arms around her waist, and nuzzled her neck. Her fists balled when purple braids turned around and put her arms around his neck, and they kissed a long, passionate kiss. Without letting her coworkers know what was going on, Reeva stood up.

"I'll be right back," she said and headed for the bar.

As she fought her way through the crowd, Reeva continued to watch the pair in each other's faces, smiling and laughing the same way he had with her just a few days before. By the time she reached the bar, Reeva was furious with him and angry with herself for thinking that Richmond had real affection for her. She tapped him on the shoulder, and he turned to her. His eyes opened wide.

"Hello, Richmond."

"Reeva."

"Goodbye, Richmond," Reeva said and walked away. Richmond went after her.

The woman with the purple braids looked on, incensed that the man she was in love with just left her standing there while he ran after another woman. She looked at the woman and remembered seeing her at the Lit Lounge.

"Reeva, Reeva, stop," Richmond said and grabbed her arm.

She broke free of his grip. "What do you want, Richmond?"

"It's not what you think," Richmond said.

"Whatever," she said and started walking. He grabbed her again. "Let me go," she said, once again freeing herself from his grip.

"We're just friends."

Reeva got in his face. "Y'all look like more than friends with your tongue down her throat," she said and started to walk away again, and once again, Richmond grabbed her arm. This time she wheeled around and slapped him in the face. "Fuck you," she said, walking away, and this time, Richmond didn't try to stop her.

Reeva went back to the table and sat down with her co-workers. She felt hurt, humiliated, and embarrassed. She was glad when nobody said anything about her exchange with Richmond. If they didn't see it, it didn't happen, and she wasn't going to tell them.

"I'm gonna go on and get outta here. I got a splitting headache," Reeva said, and she stood up. When she did, Lenecia stood up too. "No, Lenecia, you stay. Have a good time."

"You sure?"

"Yes, I'm sure. You have fun, and I will see you guys on Monday," she said, grabbing her purse.

"Okay, if you're sure you'll be all right," Lenecia said and sat down. "I hope you feel better."

"I will, thanks."

"Good night, Reeva," Cheryl said.

"See you Monday," Sharonda said as a man asked her to dance.

"Good night," Reeva said, waving as she walked away from the table toward the front door.

"Excuse me, Reeva?" a man said as she passed, and Reeva stopped.

"Clayton?" she said when she recognized him. His name was Clayton Dell. He and Reeva used to work together when she was shipping manager at Titanium Distributing Service. "How are you?"

"I'm fine, Reeva. How are you doing?"

"I'm okay," she said tentatively because he used to work at Titanium. *First Daniel and now Clayton?* Reeva questioned. *It's not a coincidence.*

"I don't want to take up a lot of your time, but did Elias Colton give you something to keep for him?" Dell asked.

"What is it with you people? No, I haven't seen or talked to Elias in years." Reeva shook her head in disgust. "Daniel sent you, didn't he?"

Dell shrugged his shoulders. "He reached out to me. Said it was important. I told him I'd ask."

Reeva paused to think for a second. "Did you follow me here?"

"No. Well, yeah, kinda."

She pointed in his face. "You people need to leave me the fuck alone!" Reeva shouted angrily over the music and walked away.

When she got outside, Reeva stood there for a second or two thinking about Richmond, fighting back the urge to cry. Then she shook it off. "His loss," she said and headed for her car.

Reeva was almost there when she thought that she heard a noise coming from behind her. She stopped and looked around, and when she didn't see anybody, Reeva turned.

That was when she heard the shot.

Reeva Duckworth was pronounced dead at the scene.